"All you have to do is relax," Kayla teased

"Relax?" Brett tried to laugh, but it turned into a groan when she slipped her hands under his shirt and ran them up his torso. "You can't be serious." He choked out the words.

In response, Kayla pushed up his shirt, pulled it over his head and threw it carelessly to the floor. "Then just stay still," she murmured.

"That's asking a lot…." He breathed in sharply as she leaned forward and attached her lips—and teeth—to his bare nipple.

"Maybe," she whispered, blowing softly, letting her warm breath soothe his skin. "But trust me. You'll be rewarded for your compliance." She leaned back and looked at him, her desire obvious. "Okay, time for the pants."

While he unzipped his jeans as quickly as he could, given his straining erection, he said, "Anyone ever told you you're kind of bossy?"

"I prefer to think of myself as a take-charge kind of girl. One who's not afraid to go after what she wants."

Then with a gleam in her eye, she reached for him. "And what I *want* right now is to pay you back for that fabulous orgasm you just gave me…."

Blaze™

Dear Reader,

I'll admit it—I'm a girly girl. I like high heels and lipstick and getting dressed up. But I also like the thrill of stepping outside my comfort zone and trying something new, like the thrilling ATV and Zodiac boat adventures I recently enjoyed. For me, the trick for choosing these new adventures is knowing my limits and not attempting anything *too* extreme. Translation: I'd love to take a walking tour across England, but you'll never see me jumping out of a plane.

In *Just Trust Me*... Kayla Watson is about to find out what happens when she decides to step outside her girly-girl box and embark on a Big Adventure. Problem is, it seems she's made the mistake of taking on a bit too much, in both the form of her extreme vacation and the very unexpected and sexy Brett Thornton. But she'll have to discover her limits on her own—along with a few surprising things about herself. Let the games begin!

I love to hear from readers, and would love to hear about *your* Big Adventure! You can contact me through my Web site at www.JacquieD.com, where you can find out about all my latest news.

Happy reading and adventuring,

Jacquie D'Alessandro

JACQUIE D'ALESSANDRO

Just Trust Me...

TORONTO • NEW YORK • LONDON
AMSTERDAM • PARIS • SYDNEY • HAMBURG
STOCKHOLM • ATHENS • TOKYO • MILAN • MADRID
PRAGUE • WARSAW • BUDAPEST • AUCKLAND

ISBN-13: 978-0-373-79280-1
ISBN-10: 0-373-79280-8

JUST TRUST ME...

This edition published by arrangement with Harlequin Books S.A.

www.eHarlequin.com

Printed in U.S.A.

ABOUT THE AUTHOR

Growing up on Long Island, New York, *USA TODAY* bestselling author Jacquie D'Alessandro fell in love with romance at an early age. She dreamed of being swept away by a dashing rogue riding a spirited stallion. When her hero finally showed up, he was dressed in jeans and drove a Volkswagen, but she recognized him anyway. They married after both graduating from Hofstra University and are now living their happily-ever-afters in Atlanta, Georgia, along with their very bright and active son, who is a dashing rogue in the making. Although a self-avowed "girly girl," Jacquie was recently spotted on both an ATV waterfall adventure and a Zodiac boat dodging huge ocean waves. Those screams you heard were shouts of pure joy. *Really.* When Jacquie isn't recovering from her latest adventure, she loves to hear from readers. You can contact her through her Web site at www.JacquieD.com.

Books by Jacquie D'Alessandro

HARLEQUIN BLAZE

200—WHY NOT TONIGHT?

HARLEQUIN TEMPTATION

917—IN OVER HIS HEAD
954—A SURE THING?
999—WE'VE GOT TONIGHT

This book is dedicated with love and gratitude to the wonderful, supportive people of PBE who came to my Melbourne book signing and made me feel so special. Thank you to Cheryl Heuer, Mary King, Sue Moody, Nancy Barry, Alice Dunne and Kay and Jim Johnson for giving me such a wonderful day.

And to my editor, Brenda Chin, whose zest for adventure inspired this story.

And as always, to my wonderful husband, Joe, who makes every day a Big Adventure, and my beautiful son, Christopher, aka Big Adventure Junior.

Prologue

KAYLA WATSON hurried through the Miami airport, cursing the high heels that prevented her from breaking into a dead run. Of course her gate was at the very end of this seemingly endless concourse. Damn it, if she missed her flight—

She cut off the thought, refusing to consider the havoc that would wreak with her already insane schedule. Her cell phone rang and she shot it an impatient glance, grimacing when the name *Nelson Sigler* showed on the caller ID. As much as she didn't feel like talking to her boss at the moment, he *was* the CEO and expected her to answer the phone when he called.

"How'd the photo shoot go?" Nelson asked without preamble.

Exhausting. But, as the director of public relations at the New York office of La Fleur, the world's most innovative cosmetics company, Kayla was well-acquainted with putting a positive spin on things. Especially head ache-inducing photo shoots that pitted cranky, moody models against impatient, moody photographers.

"Fine," she answered, forcing a cheery note into her voice as she wove through the crowd. "The photos will be fabulous. Perfect for the new ad campaign." Right. Just don't ask how much finessing and cajoling and feather-smoothing it took to make certain of that.

"Good. No problem with Alicia?"

The mere mention of the petulant model's name made Kayla's eye twitch. Alicia possessed a million-dollar face—and a diva streak the size of North America. She showed up late for her bookings, and was difficult when she finally did arrive. Which was why the photo session had run late. Which is why sweat now oozed down Kayla's spine as she hurried to make her flight.

"Everything with Alicia worked out perfectly," she told Nelson in a soothing voice.

"Excellent. You sound out of breath."

"The shoot ran a bit long and I'm dashing to make my flight. I'll see you at the office tomorrow."

She'd no sooner disconnected than the loudspeaker warned, "Final boarding call for flight 254 to New York."

Many gates and travelers still stood between her and her flight. Too many. Reaching down, she yanked off her heels and ran. When she arrived at the gate five minutes later, barefoot, sweating, breathless, the gate agent said, "I'm sorry, you missed the flight. But I'll be happy to re-book you on the next one. It departs in two hours."

Swallowing her frustration, Kayla thanked the woman, then, with her new boarding pass in hand, she flopped into the nearest seat, her mind spinning with the various appointments she'd need to reschedule courtesy of this delay—when all she really wanted to do was take some aspirin for her pounding stress headache and go to sleep.

With a sigh, she reached down to slip her shoes back on, and her gaze fell on an issue of *U.S. Weekly Review* magazine a previous traveler had left on the chair next to hers. She read the bold-print headline: *Stressed? Out Of Balance? No Change, No Gain!*

A short, humorless sound escaped her. Between her job, helping to plan her older sister's wedding, dealing with the drama that was her younger sister's life, her matchmaking mother and what seemed to be a never-ending string of miserable dates, *stressed* and *out of balance* perfectly described the chaotic whirlwind her life had become over the past year.

She glanced around at the nearby travelers. Most seemed to be business people, talking on cell phones, tapping on laptops, all engrossed in their own little world, oblivious to everything and everyone around them, frowning, looking stressed. Is this what she'd become? Unfortunately, it seemed so.

With a sigh, she picked up the magazine and settled back to read the article. By the time she'd finished, Kayla felt emotionally drained, yet at the same time elated, renewed and filled with purpose. The article's dead-on descriptions of the discontent and frustrations she'd been experiencing both personally and professionally made it seem as if the words were written expressly for her.

Yes, she was stressed. Yes, she lacked balance in her life. And according to the article, if she didn't shake things up, step out her comfort zone, things would only get worse. No change, no gain.

Her gaze settled on the handwritten testimonial scribbled in ink at the end of the article, obviously by the magazine's previous owner: "This changed my life. I hope it does the same for you."

Kayla closed the magazine and held it against her chest. She hoped so, too. Because she badly needed a change.

1

"YOU WANT ME to go *where?* To do *what?* With *whom?*"

After uttering those questions, Kayla stared at Nelson. Until thirty seconds ago, she'd thought her boss was a rational human being. Clearly, however, the man was insane.

Nelson stared right back at her over the tops of his bifocals. "To Peru. To spy. On Brett Thornton."

Brett Thornton. Kayla barely managed to suppress a grimace. How was it possible to so thoroughly dislike a man she'd never even met? In the course of only four months, he'd become the bane of her existence. She was well accustomed to dealing with everything from the media to demanding executives to high-maintenance, diva-like models. Who would have thought that some unknown nerdy *scientist* could prove such a problem?

"I flunked Spying 101," she said with a breezy laugh. "So clearly I'm not the best choice."

"You *are* the best choice," Nelson said in the deep, implacable tone Kayla recognized all too well after working for him for the past ten years. It was the tone that indicated he'd made up his mind and there'd be no changing it. "Thornton's claims of developing an anti-aging formula that will not only render cosmetic surgery obsolete but has aphrodisiac qualities, as well, is the cutting edge we need."

"Unfortunately every other cosmetics company in the world feels the same way."

"Exactly. Which is why I want to make sure La Fleur has the upper hand right from the beginning. We lost out two years ago on that new sunless-tan formula. We're not losing again."

"But Thornton's been dangling that golden carrot for four months and hasn't produced yet."

"Doesn't mean he won't."

She made a disgusted sound. "My personal opinion is that he's loving all the attention every cosmetics firm—including us—is lavishing on him. Basking in the perks, the wining, dining and wooing—he's milking it for all it's worth, and when it finally comes time to put out his so-called miracle product, he'll have nothing."

"That is a possibility," Nelson agreed. "But it's also just as likely he's being cautious, and as aggravating as that is, I can't blame him. If his claims are true, the product will revolutionize not only skin care but foreplay as well. Who could resist such a product? You know as well as I do that sex sells. And La Fleur *will* own the product."

There was no need for him add "or else"—it was fully implied. And certainly if Thornton's claims were true, Kayla wanted La Fleur to own the miracle formula. But after months with no physical proof, she had serious doubts as to whether Thornton's claims were valid.

And then there was her personal dislike of the man. While she'd been spared dealing with him personally, her staff had not been so fortunate, reporting that

Thornton was standoffish, refused interviews and didn't return phone calls. Bad enough—but her one near-encounter with him two months ago had convinced her he lacked any redeeming qualities.

She'd spent weeks arranging a fabulous party in Thornton's honor to introduce him to key La Fleur people, seen to it that every mover and shaker in New York had been invited, along with a host of local celebrities and all the La Fleur models. And what did Brett Thornton do? He'd abruptly left—without a word, before the party had barely begun. And before he'd been introduced to the managerial team, herself included. Furious and appalled by his rudeness, she'd been forced to improvise a plausible excuse to the company's president, CFO and board of directors who looked to her to explain why the guest of honor was MIA.

Just thinking about it now fueled her anger all over again. As far as she was concerned, Brett Thornton—oops, sorry—*Dr.* Thornton as he'd insisted upon being called—was more of a headache than a roomful of hungover supermodels. He was just another arrogant overnight sensation who courted media interest, then turned into a first-class whiner about the "intrusive" attention. Exactly the sort of person she most disliked.

Nelson slid a sheet of paper toward her over his lake-sized glass-topped desk. "Here's your itinerary. Your flight to Lima leaves at nine o'clock. That gives you plenty of time to go home and—"

"Whoa, hold it," Kayla said, extending her hand like a stop sign. "Nine o'clock *tonight?*" Good grief, she hadn't even unpacked from yesterday's re-booked Miami flight.

"Tonight," Nelson confirmed.

Everything inside Kayla groaned. In an effort to save herself, she said, "I'm attending the launch for the Hidden Secrets fragrance line tomorrow—"

"I've reassigned that to Caroline," Nelson interjected, naming Kayla's senior publicist. "She can handle your calendar until you return."

"Caroline—or someone else on my staff—can just as easily make this trip to woo Thornton."

Nelson shook his head. "You're missing the point. This trip isn't about wooing or schmoozing. It's about gathering information—discreetly. I want to know why he's going to *Peru,* of all places."

Kayla's curiosity was piqued in spite of herself. "You think it has something to do with his formula? That maybe there's a secret ingredient in some plant found only in South America?"

"Maybe. If the man merely wanted a vacation, why not just go to the Caribbean or Hawaii or even Europe? Why Peru?"

"You have a point—it is a bit off the beaten track."

"That's what I thought. Especially since it's obvious he's gone to great pains to keep this trip secret."

"How did you find out about it?"

Nelson treated her to a razor-sharp smile. "I'm not at liberty to say. Suffice it to know that my source is impeccable."

"And how do you know that Lancôme and Estée Lauder and all our other competitors aren't sending spies to Peru, as well?"

"I don't, but I'd lay odds that no one else knows about Thornton's plans. It was just by a stroke of freakish luck that *I* found out about them. Worst-case scenario is that the competition will be there, too, in which case, I'd need you there to run interference and represent our interests. But my gut tells me that won't be the case and that this is the perfect opportunity for us to learn more. Not just about the formula and its properties, but the man himself. All without him realizing it's being done, especially by someone connected to La Fleur. Which is one reason why Caroline is out—she's met Thornton."

"What about April or Ted?" she asked, naming two more of her staff.

"No. Ted met Thornton last week. You're the best, and the best is what's required for this trip."

Part of her was flattered at Nelson's recognition of her job skills. But another part—the part that had lately grumbled with discontent over some of the things she'd done to be the best—was less than pleased. "Thank you, but April is very competent and she's never met Thornton."

"She has back problems."

Kayla frowned. "What does that have to do with anything?"

"The trip would be too vigorous for her."

"Vigorous?" Her eyes narrowed with suspicion. "What sort of trip is this? Some kind of rafting expedition down the anaconda-filled Amazon?"

Nelson looked insulted. "Of course not. I know you don't like snakes."

"Amen to that."

"Besides, you'd need yellow fever shots for the Amazon."

She blinked. "It scares me that you even know that."

"Not to worry. This trip is perfectly safe and doesn't involve the Amazon at all. I know what a girly girl you are."

"Uh-huh. And this seems like a good time to remind you that there's nothing wrong with that. This *is* a cosmetics company after all—not Extreme Sports-R-Us."

Nelson smiled. "Not to worry—"

"The fact that that's the second time you've said that in the last ten seconds is *not* reassuring. Exactly what sort of trip is this?"

"You want the good news or the bad news first?"

"Oh, God." She squeezed her eyes shut for several seconds, took a bracing breath, then said, "Good news. I definitely could use some good news."

"The good news is that the hotel where you're scheduled to stay in Aguas Calientes is incredible. Breathtaking views, gourmet food, five-star treatment all the way."

"And the bad news?"

"It's a four-day hike to Aguas Calientes."

A deafening silence filled the room. When Kayla finally found her voice, she said, *"Hike?"*

"Hike. Aguas Calientes is the town nearest to Machu Picchu, the lost city of the Incas in the Andes mountains. You'll enjoy a four-day hike along the famous Inca trail to the ruins, which are reputed to be spectacular. Then, at the end of the journey, you'll be pampered at the Sanctuary Lodge which is the height of luxury."

"You sound like a travel agent."

"Just trying to focus on the positives. And it's not as grueling as it sounds."

"That's a relief, because I must tell you, a four-*hour* hike sounds grueling. A four-*day* hike sounds…insane."

"You'll have a guide and porters who carry the tents and cooking gear."

"Tents and cooking gear are the *positives?*" She shook her head. "Limos and facials and sun-drenched tropical beaches are positives."

"You'll be fine. I recall you once mentioning you were a Girl Scout."

"Yes. When I was *ten.* Nowadays, I'm afraid my idea of roughing it is staying at a Holiday Inn instead of a Hyatt."

"You have a gym membership. You can handle this."

"I'm not worried about my ability to hike up the mountain. But neither yoga, spinning nor Pilates prepare one for sleeping in the wild outdoors. In tents."

"Think of this as an opportunity to do something new for a change. To step outside the box."

Nelson's words halted her, and she immediately recalled the article she'd read yesterday. *No Change, No Gain.* According to the article, if she always did what she'd always done, she'd always be where she'd always been. To get her life back in balance, she needed to challenge herself. Step outside her box. Go somewhere she'd never been, and do something she'd never done.

No doubt about it, a four-day, tent-sleeping, gear-lugging, outdoor-roughing-it hike in the Andes qualified for waaay outside her box. She'd been thinking more along the lines of a spa trip to St. Bart's for a seaweed wrap—something she'd never done in a place she'd never been.

But even she had to admit that such pampering wouldn't qualify as "challenging." Was it fate that had Nelson scheduling her for this trip? *Let's hope so,* her inner voice whispered. Right. As opposed to it being a bone-breaking, nightmarish, hikers-eaten-by-giant-snakes coincidence. Which probably just proved that this trip *was* fate. A mighty, between-the-shoulder-blades shove outside her comfort zone. One that, based on her St. Bart's spa idea, she sure as hell wouldn't have planned on her own. And one that was exactly what she needed.

In fact, if Dr. Brett Thornton wasn't in the mix, everything would be perfect. Or at least as perfect as a four-day hike up a mountain could be.

The timing, however, was not great. With Meg's wedding only a month away, her sister was bound to freak when she heard Kayla would be away for a week. Kayla took her maid-of-honor duties seriously, and she hated to leave Meg now—especially since her future in-laws were arriving this weekend from California. But unless she wanted to resign from her job here and now, she had little choice.

"Listen, Kayla, I know this is a bit outside your realm," Nelson's voice jerked her away from her thoughts, "but surely if Thornton, who no doubt spends all his time peering through microscopes, can make the hike, so can you."

"So far you've flattered me, appealed to my vanity, and now you're trying to rev up my competitive spirit."

Nelson smiled. "Is it working?"

She wanted to say no. Tell him that she was tired. Physically, emotionally exhausted. And so damn weary of doing things she didn't really want to do. Like trek to another continent to partake in what boiled down to spying on a man she had no desire to spend one minute with, let alone one week with. That between work and her crappy personal life, she was completely out of balance. But clearly Nelson wasn't going to take no for an answer, and Thornton's miracle product was too much of a temptation to ignore. As was the opportunity to exact some spy-filled revenge on the arrogant scientist. Yes, a bit of payback for the way he'd treated her staff and embarrassed her was exactly what he deserved.

She smiled. "Put me in, coach."

"That's the spirit. You're booked to spend a day in Cusco, the city where you'll overnight before departing on your hike to Machu Picchu. Maybe you can even strike up a conversation with Thornton during that time. According to our travel agency, your hotel is less than a quarter mile away from Thornton's. All the information is on your itinerary." A satisfied smile curved his lips. "The time with Thornton should give you ample opportunity to befriend him and find out what his plans are for the formula. And to make certain that La Fleur is in those plans."

Nelson rose, indicating their meeting was concluded. "I'm out of the office for the rest of day," he said, leading the way into the hallway, then turning toward the elevators. "I'll want updates on your progress, although I don't know what the cell-phone service will be like."

Nervous jitters tingled down her spine at the thought of dead air space. Maybe this was stepping too far outside her box. But then she shook off her apprehension and mentally chanted her new mantra: *No change, no gain.*

They reached the bank of elevators and Nelson pushed the down button. "Bring home the goods here, Kayla, and the La Fleur world will be your oyster. We're talking bonus, perks, another promotion."

Only a few short months ago, she'd have been thrilled by those words. Now, for reasons she didn't quite understand but that undoubtedly had to do with her life being out of balance, she felt a strong urge to tell Nelson that as far as she was concerned, oysters were nothing but icky bits of slime. Instead she smiled. "You can count on me."

"I knew I could." The elevator doors slid open and he stepped inside. "Oh, and be sure to pack some warm clothes. It's hot during the day, but I understand it can get pretty chilly on the trail at night."

The elevator door closed, and Kayla found herself staring at her own reflection in the polished brass door. She looked a little shell-shocked.

Not a big surprise, considering that's exactly how she felt.

But, according to the *U.S. Weekly Review* article, this trip was exactly what she needed. And she'd learned long ago that when life handed you lemons, you made lemonade.

Of course, in the case of a four-day hike up a mountain with a man she regarded with high suspicion, she hoped this was more a case of life handing her limes, since, thanks to Brett Thornton, she didn't doubt she'd need to make a margarita. Or two.

I understand it can get pretty chilly on the trail at night.

Three or four was definitely not out of the question.

2

SEATED AT a table at one of Cusco's numerous outdoor cafés with a bottle of sparkling water at his elbow, Brett Thornton stretched out his legs and surveyed his surroundings. A sense of calm awe settled over him. Incredible to think that mere hours ago he'd been in fast-paced Manhattan, and now he sat where the mighty Incas had lived centuries ago.

His gaze drifted over the stately Plaza de Armas, the focal point in this picturesque city referred to as the capital of the Inca empire. Drenched in bright, late-afternoon sunlight, the plaza teemed with tourists and merchants. Lined with colorful arcades and carved wooden balconies, its building foundations laid by the Incas over five centuries ago, the plaza was a sight to behold and seemed imbued with the spirit of the people who'd once roamed the stone streets.

Leaning back, he took a sip of his water, the recommended drink to help acclimate to the high altitude, and for the first time in months, felt some of the tension that had been his constant companion ease. If he'd suspected how insane his life would become after publishing his findings regarding his anti-aging aphrodisiac, he would have taken more precautions to insure his privacy. He'd figured he'd receive attention, but he'd in no way been prepared for the blitz that had ambushed him.

And not only from every cosmetics firm. Acquaintances he hadn't heard from in years suddenly wished to renew their friendship. He'd even received calls and correspondence from people claiming to be long-lost, distant relatives. Then there was the plethora of lawyers and financial advisors wanting to represent his interests, and charities asking for donations. He'd changed his number twice and disconnected his phone at work but they'd still found him. There were nearly ten thousand e-mails in his inbox.

Good God, now he knew how people who won the lottery must feel—overwhelmed and inundated. Crushed by everyone suddenly wanting a piece of the money, or in his case, the formula.

He'd happened upon the basics of the formula by accident in his home lab, but once he had, his scientific curiosity had pushed him to refine it. And after three years of research and experimentation, he was convinced it was ready to be introduced. All it had taken was publishing an article in a scientific journal, and then, like an exponential equation, the news had spread rapidly, mushrooming like a nuclear explosion. And his life hadn't been the same since.

The upside was that if the formula proved successful and he sold it, he'd be financially set for life. Definitely a huge inducement, especially for a guy living in a cramped apartment in a very untrendy section of Manhattan with another decade worth of student loans to pay. And certainly it would be nice to pay off his parents' mortgage and treat them to the sort of vacation they deserved.

The downside was that except for his folks and a few close friends, he didn't know who to trust. People and offers were coming at him from all sides. He was a scientist, not a businessman. He knew squat about negotiating deals and finalizing contracts and all the myriad things that he was suddenly required to know. He needed expert advice and over the past few months had worked on figuring out who he wanted in his camp. What he'd learned during that time was that there were a lot of shallow, greedy people in the world. And unfortunately, it seemed most of them had his phone number.

Most surprising and most hurtful of all, was the realization that Lynda fell into that shallow, greedy category. How, after being together for a year, had he not seen her true character? He'd thought them very compatible, their scientific natures completely in sync. While their relationship might have lacked some physical chemistry, he'd found their shared passion for science quite fulfilling.

He'd learned how wrong he was two months ago at a party thrown by La Fleur Cosmetics in his honor, when he'd found her on her knees, servicing a male model—a discovery which had prompted him to abruptly abandon the festivities. He hadn't been impressed with the company's aggressive campaign to lure him their way, and seeing his girlfriend's lips wrapped around their model's cock hadn't endeared them.

He grimaced then swigged his water, suddenly wishing for a beer. Damn. If only he could invent a formula that would erase *that* visual from his mind. Not that he was heartbroken. No, rather, he'd been totally shocked. And royally pissed—at her for cheating and at himself for not recognizing that she would. And with a pretty-boy model type, no less. That was the last sort of guy he'd ever have expected the very serious Dr. Lynda Maxwell to go for.

But go for him she had. In a big way. Thanks to his failed relationship with Lynda, he'd learned the hard way that dating a work colleague was not a good idea—especially after the romance ended. He'd heard through the grapevine at their laboratory at Scientific Industries that she and the model had recently jetted off to some exotic Caribbean resort. According to Lynda's own explanation of the attraction, she'd taken one look at the guy and been "hooked up to a nuclear reactor." Completely unscientific and ridiculous.

But between Lynda and the constant pressure and people and companies trying to woo him, he'd had enough. He needed peace. Quiet. Away from everyone and everything pulling him in so many directions he couldn't even concentrate on his work. In a place where no one knew him. In a location that would cleanse him, body and soul, of the craziness that had wrapped itself around every facet of his life with a chokehold. A place where he could get back to basics and find inner peace. Somewhere plain and simple. Filled with history and a sense of legend. A step back in time.

There'd been no doubt in his mind where he'd wanted to go. Traveling to Cusco, then hiking from the gateway city to Machu Picchu had been a sojourn he'd wanted to take for years, ever since studying the Inca empire in high school. The Inca people, their society and culture, had fascinated him. Unfortunately college and life had prevented him from making the trip, but the desire to go had remained bubbling in the back of his mind.

And now he hadn't allowed anything to stop him from taking the journey. Because now it wasn't just a case of *wanting* to make the trip—he *needed* to do so. He'd use this time away to renew himself and reflect and when he returned to New York, he'd be prepared to deal with the future of his formula.

He finished off his bottle of water and was looking around for the waiter to order another when his attention was caught by a woman walking toward him across the plaza. Huge dark glasses and a floppy straw hat obscured most of her face. But it wasn't her face that riveted his attention. No, it was the sinfully sinuous way she moved—combined with the fact that the sun's bright rays slanting behind her rendered her gauzy, ankle-length skirt nearly transparent.

Whoa, baby. And what a view it was.

He sat up straighter, mesmerized by how the transparent material outlined her outrageously curvy hips and long, shapely legs. His mouth went dry and he instantly fantasized about what, if anything, she wore beneath her skirt. With every step closer, his temperature notched up another degree. He was surprised she didn't leave a trail of smoke behind her. His gaze flicked upward, noting a bright turquoise tank top that showed off toned arms and a hint of cleavage. When he'd planned this trip, the last thing on his mind had been women—other than wanting to get away from the ones fawning over him because of his formula.

But one look at smokin' hot Miss Transparent Skirt sure as hell had women racing to the forefront of his mind. And this woman in particular. Along with the reminder that he hadn't been with anyone since Lynda. And in a single heartbeat, this woman made him want to banish the phrase *hadn't been with anyone lately* from his vocabulary. With an intensity that surprised him. The last time he'd been so instantly smitten with a woman, especially just on the basis of her looks, was…never.

A cloud drifted across the sun, ending his unexpected view. "Damn," he muttered. He reached into his pocket, intending to toss some centavos on the table to pay for his water then go after her, but he realized she was heading toward the café where he sat. Sitting back, he adopted a nonchalant pose and from behind his sunglasses watched her sit down several tables away. Before he could strike up a conversation, however, she reached into her canvas tote bag, withdrew a magazine, and promptly opened it and started reading.

His gaze drifted idly over her reading material and halted. *U.S Weekly Review.* His favorite magazine, which, along with its like-minded competitor, *Newsweek,* was the only publication outside the scientific community he religiously read. He took particular note because the issue she held was one which contained a very inspirational article on stress and balancing your life. The article's catchphrase flashed in his mind: *No change, no gain*—a bit of advice he'd taken to heart. Advice that had inspired him to finally get off his ass and make this trip.

At that moment, the waiter approached her and she lowered the magazine. Thanks to her huge dark glasses and floppy straw hat, all he could tell was that she had a great smile, one which clearly dazzled the waiter. And, after hearing her order a bottle of water, that she sounded distinctly American.

Now that his brain cells were no longer stupefied by her transparent skirt, he decided she was most likely here with someone, a husband no doubt, although a quick glance at her left hand showed she wore no ring. Okay, so a boyfriend. One who probably had a black belt and was on his way to the café right now.

Just then, she looked directly at him—or at least he thought she did. It was hard to tell with those crazy huge sunglasses. And she smiled. Although her transparent skirt was a tough act to follow, that smile did a damn decent job.

Just in case a black-belt boyfriend hovered in the area, he turned his head left then right, then took a peek over his shoulder. As there was no one else around him, he concluded her smile was meant for him, which greatly pleased him, although sort of surprised him. While he'd had his fair share of girlfriends and lovers, he'd never describe himself as a babe magnet. In his experience, not all women found his everyday look of goggles and dingy lab coat sexy. Discounting, of course, the models who'd draped themselves over him at the numerous gatherings recently thrown in his honor by the various cosmetics firms vying for his attention. But then he hadn't been wearing his goggles or lab coat at those functions. Still, he normally wasn't the guy hot women flocked to at parties.

Maybe because you never go to parties, his inner voice interjected. *When you did, look at all those gorgeous, hot models who'd wanted a piece of you.*

Not him, he reminded himself. His formula. A sobering reality check.

But this woman didn't know anything about his formula. That smile was just for him. And that felt damn good.

He smiled back, and she asked, "Do you speak English?"

Her voice was soft and slightly husky, as if she'd just rolled out of bed. His imagination conjured up an image of her long legs tangled in his sheets, and heat that had nothing to do with the bright sun sizzled through him.

"Only when I want someone to understand what I'm saying," he said.

She laughed, a sexy, smoky sound that resonated through him and vibrated all his nerve endings to attention. "I thought you might be American," she said.

"Why's that?"

"Your shirt."

He looked down at the colorful, short-sleeved tropical-print shirt he'd left unbuttoned over his T-shirt. "Are you saying my Hawaiian print screams American tourist?"

"Loud and clear. Not that there's anything wrong with that. Based on your accent, I'm guessing you're from the northeast."

"New York."

Her smile widened and she leaned forward, resting her elbows on the small, round ceramic table. "Really? Me, too. I live in Manhattan."

He huffed out a surprised breath. "Small world. So do I. Lower West Side."

"Upper East Side."

He didn't doubt it for a minute. He couldn't see much of her, but what he could see—the bright smile, the toned arms and shoulders to match her obviously toned legs, the glasses, hat and sandals he guessed bore designer logos and were the height of fashion—looked pampered and expensive. Definitely high-maintenance. Just the sort of woman who wasn't his type. Just the sort of woman who'd been fawning over him lately at every cosmetic company function he'd attended. Just the sort of woman who represented everything he was trying to avoid.

Yet even as his better judgment reminded him of that, along with the fact that he had enough trouble in his life right now trying to focus on the biggest career decision he'd ever faced without throwing a woman—*any* woman—into the mix, his libido had him asking, "So what brings you to Cusco?"

She made a breathy noise that sounded self-conscious. "You'll think I'm crazy, but I'm here because of an article I read in this magazine." She held up the copy of *U.S. Weekly Review.* "It's about rebalancing your life."

Brett's brows shot up. *"No Change, No Gain?"*

There was no mistaking her surprise. "That's right! You've read it?"

Okay, maybe he wasn't looking for female companionship, but how could he possibly ignore a woman who was not only smokin' hot, but also clearly a kindred spirit? "Would you believe that it's part of the reason I'm here?"

She laughed. "Considering the fact that it induced *me* to come here and hike up the Andes to Machu Picchu—something that's so outside my comfort zone as to be laughable, yes, I'd believe it. You weren't kidding when you said 'small world.'"

Before he could reply, the waiter returned with her bottle of water. After setting it down, the young man approached Brett's table.

"Another, *señor?*" the young man asked, picking up Brett's empty bottle.

"Please." After the waiter moved off, Brett studied her for several seconds and couldn't deny he liked what he saw. A lot. Her unmistakable uptown aura rendered her Ms. Wrong, but the sex appeal rippling off her and grabbing him by the throat—and groin—rendered her Ms. Right Now. So, while she wasn't what he needed for the long term, the tightening ache in his boxers strongly indicated she was definitely what he wanted for the short term. The fact they were on the same *no change, no gain* wavelength just sealed the deal.

"Would you care to join me?" he asked.

She hesitated for several seconds, and he figured she was debating whether or not he might be a serial killer. Clearly she decided he wasn't because she said, "Sure. No point in talking across the tables."

She rose and, after picking up her magazine, tote bag and bottle of water, wove her way around the trio of tables separating them with the same sinuous grace with which she'd crossed the plaza. His eyes shielded by his own sunglasses, Brett's gaze skimmed down her shapely, feminine form, from her tank top to the flat sandals decorated with colorful jeweled flowers that adorned her feet, and awareness jolted through him. No doubt about it, she'd lit his fire without even trying. She slid into the chair opposite his and set down her things.

"Thanks for the invite," she said with a half smile, drawing his attention to her full lips which looked even better up close and glistened with a touch of something glossy. Holding out her hand, she said, "I'm Kayla

Watson. Stressed, out-of-balance New Yorker hoping to be rehabilitated."

He shook her hand, noting her firm, businesslike grip, along with the fact that her skin felt remarkably soft. "Nice to meet you, Kayla," he said, holding on to her hand a fraction longer than was necessary before releasing her. "Brett Thornton. Another stressed, out-of-balance New Yorker." He inhaled and her scent wafted across to him, all but intoxicating him.

"Your fragrance," he murmured. "Coconut. And a hint of lime..." He inhaled again. "Some sort of flower." And something else that was uniquely her.

In spite of her large glasses, there was no missing her surprise. "The flower is gardenia. So what are you—some sort of perfume tester?"

"No. Just have a keen sense of smell." He smiled. "Especially when it comes to women with beautiful smiles who smell like delicious tropical drinks with flowers floating in them." As he spoke, he found himself wishing she'd remove her glasses and hat so he could see her face. He wanted to know if the rest of her packed as powerful a wallop as her smile.

And her transparent skirt.

"Thanks, but I'd think most men would describe a tropical drink with flowers floating in it as girly or frou-frou. Delicious? Not a chance. Makes me wonder what you do for a living—since it's not perfume tester."

A sense of relaxation eased through Brett. Damn, but it felt good to be with someone who didn't know. Who didn't want something from him. Leaning back in his chair, he grinned. "Guess."

The waiter arrived with his water, and after he'd departed she said, "Hit man?"

"Because I look like a murderer?"

"No. Because I think it's important to rule out occupations like that, especially if we're going to share a café table."

"Not a hit man," he assured her, "although I'd hardly admit it if I were."

"Noted. How about a chef? They need a good sense of smell."

"I can barely fry an egg."

He felt her gaze roam over him. "Your hands look strong. And clever. Artist?"

Blood shot to his groin at the thought of showing her just how clever his hands could be. "Can only draw stick figures."

"Wine-taster?"

"No, but that sounds like a great job. Where do I apply?"

She laughed. "Bartender?"

"Because they're known for their keen sense of smell?"

"No, because you're easy to talk to."

"Thanks, but seeing as how I'm the only one here to talk to, I'm not sure that's much of a compliment."

"I meant it as one."

"I bet you say that to all the out-of-balance New Yorkers you meet in Cusco."

She grinned. "Caught." She tapped her chin with a fingertip. "Fisherman?"

"Do I smell briny?"

"Not that I can tell. But I figured a fisherman would need to differentiate between cod and salmon and mahi mahi. That sort of thing."

"I wouldn't know a mahi mahi if it jumped up and bit my butt."

"I didn't know mahi mahi had teeth."

He laughed. "They probably don't. I wouldn't know. Give up?"

"Not yet." She appeared to give him the once-over. "Your obvious fondness for Hawaiian shirts rules out any career in the fashion industry—"

"Hey, I'll have you know I bought this from a guy selling clothes out of the back of a truck on Madison Avenue."

"I like your shirt just fine. I'm just saying the folks over at Ralph Lauren and Calvin Klein probably wouldn't. Back to my guessing—you appear to be in good shape...carpenter?"

"Nope."

"Forest ranger?"

"'Fraid not."

"Banker? Lawyer? Realtor? Mechanic?"

He couldn't help but chuckle at her rapid-fire guesses. "No to all."

"Fine. I officially give up."

"Hmmm. I wouldn't have pegged you for a quitter."

She lifted her chin. "There's a difference between quitting and strategically knowing when to throw in the towel."

"I see. It's a matter of timing."

"Exactly."

"In that case, I'll let you off the hook. I'm a scientist. I'm accustomed in my work to using my sense of smell to distinguish between chemicals and compounds, none of which are normally coconut and lime."

"I don't think I've ever met a scientist before."

"That's because they don't let us out of the laboratory very often."

"What precisely does a scientist do?"

"Research mostly. I also do some teaching."

"I have to admit I'd never have guessed. I thought scientists had wild electrocuted-looking hair and crazed gleams in their eyes."

"That's only the *mad* scientists. They get all the good movie roles." He heaved an exaggerated sigh. "The relatively sane ones, like me, are always passed over by those Hollywood types."

"Hmmm. But for all I know, your sunglasses might be hiding a crazed gleam in your eyes."

Brett suspected his eyes were indeed gleaming. Not with madness, but with unmistakable heated stirrings of lust. He wasn't sure if it was the heady sense of having escaped New York, or the magic that seemed to shimmer in the air in this ancient city, or the delicious scent and smile and laughter of the woman sitting across from him, or the fire her transparent skirt had lit, or hell, even the high altitude, but for the first time in a long while he felt…free. Relaxed. And very attracted to a woman whose face remained half-hidden.

"There's only way to find out if my shades are hiding anything," he said softly. He rested his forearms on the table and leaned forward in invitation. "Take them off. See for yourself."

3

KAYLA HESITATED, relegated, for reasons she couldn't fully explain, to mute stillness by his husky-voiced invitation. Other than to know it surprised her. As had he since he'd first smiled at her.

He wasn't at all what she'd expected, either in looks or demeanor. Based on his two interviews she'd read—before he'd ceased granting them—industry scuttlebutt, her own staff's difficulties in making any inroads with the man, and the way he'd rudely ditched his party, she'd predicted a pompous, stuffed-shirt jerk. Instead he was warm and funny and friendly.

And based on the several grainy news photos she'd seen, she'd expected a scrawny, nerdy geek. But clearly the man was just unphotogenic, because while he wasn't in the same league as the male models with whom her job put her in contact, he by no means appeared unattractive.

No, in fact, he had a really nice smile—sort of lopsided and quirky. And cute. And a rugged, square jaw. And what appeared to be a downright impressive physique hiding under his Hawaiian shirt and T-shirt. Certainly his arms looked nice, as did the breadth of his shoulders. And his thick, dark, rumpled hair begged her fingers to test its wavy texture. In fact, when she'd first seen him, she'd almost believed he was the wrong man. It wasn't until he'd actually introduced himself that she'd been certain he was the person she sought.

And now, faced with the opportunity to remove his sunglasses and unmask him, she felt an odd combination of curiosity and inexplicable nervousness. It hadn't once occurred to her that this man she'd been sent to spy on, to whom she'd relished giving a bit of ditch-the-party-and-leave-me-holding-the-bag payback might be in any way likable or attractive.

Pulling in a bracing breath she was frankly surprised she needed, she reached out, lightly grasped the black frames, then slowly lowered her hands. And stared. Into the most compelling, intense brown eyes she'd ever seen.

Those eyes, gilded with intriguing flecks of gold, seemed to laser through the protection of her glasses. His gaze was mesmerizing and sucked her in like a pool of quicksand. *Whew.* This extremely attractive man was definitely *not* what she'd expected to see. And in spite of the fact that she wasn't fond of surprises, she couldn't deny that she very much liked what she saw.

Intelligence and humor gleamed in those golden-brown depths. Along with interest. Very definite interest. Of the very heated variety. Awareness tingled under her skin, and she fought the sudden surge to fan herself. For several long seconds she simply stared at him, unable to look away, her gaze roaming his features, noting the fine grain of his skin. The shaded beginnings of a five o'clock shadow. His well defined lips that somehow looked both firm and soft. And very, very kissable. Was it possible that a reclusive science geek who undoubtedly spent all his time in a lab peering through microscopes and examining test tubes, or whatever scientists did, could be as good a kisser as his gorgeous mouth would suggest?

"Well?" he asked softly.

That single word yanked her from her thoughts. Her very inappropriate thoughts. She needed to recall that she didn't like this man. And that she was on a fact-finding mission—and not of the how-does-he-kiss variety.

Unfortunately, as she'd lost the entire thread of the conversation, she was forced to ask, "Well what?"

"Any sign of a crazed gleam?"

"A gleam...maybe. Crazed? I don't think so."

"The gleam's all your fault, you know." A slow smile curved up one corner of his gorgeous mouth, denting a dimple that could only be described as sexy in his cheek. "I'm positive it wasn't there until you showed up."

Yikes. This man and his damn dimple and damn brown eyes were *potent.* Like a shot of tequila on an empty stomach. Forcing a light tone, she matched his earlier words. "I bet you say that to all the out-of-balance New Yorkers you meet."

His smile faded and his gaze flicked down to her lips. "Actually, right now I can't imagine saying it to anyone else but you."

She'd been around the block enough times to know when she was being fed a line, and her first instinct was to believe he was full of crap. But something in his voice, in the way he was looking at her, as if he, too, was surprised by what he saw and liked it very much, shoved her cynical thoughts aside. Something was clicking here between them, something electric and exciting...wasn't it? It sure felt like it to her—in a way that had nothing to do with formulas or La Fleur or her spying mission. Obviously the high altitude was affecting her brain, but hey, if he was attracted to her, so much the better. It certainly would make getting him to open up to her that much easier.

Yet even as the thought occurred to her, her conscience tossed a cold bucket of guilt on her. While she'd been okay with the idea of covertly seeking information from the unlikable *Dr. Thornton,* trying to pry information from the very personable *Brett* suddenly felt like… lying. And she didn't care for it one bit.

So the guy makes a good first impression—in person, her inner voice chimed in. Big deal. Before today—heck, before fifteen minutes ago, he was the bane of her existence. Reclusive, unavailable, standoffish, arrogant—tossing his credentials around as if he were casting pearls before swine. Embarrassing her by ditching the party in his honor she'd planned. Playing coy and pitting every cosmetics firm in the country against each other. For a product that most likely didn't even exist. There was every chance this guy was a big fat fraud.

Right. So what if he was surprisingly attractive and had a killer smile, sexy dimples and compelling eyes? Thanks to La Fleur, she had access to dozens of male models who were a hundred times more attractive than him. Of course, they were all either jerks or had significant others or were gay. But still.

Hmmm…but still…there *was* something about Brett Thornton that shivered a heated tingle through her—something she hadn't felt in a very long time. And had never felt so strongly after such a short acquaintance. A tingle that made it nearly impossible to remember who he was and why she was here.

Indeed, meeting him here in this foreign city felt suspiciously like one of those precious and rare instances. A Meant-to-Be Moment. Her common sense immediately rejected the idea, but her humming libido definitely accepted it. And surely the fact that he'd been inspired by the same *No Change, No Gain* article as she indicated some sort of strong connection between them.

"Any chance you'd return the favor and let me take off *your* sunglasses?" he asked softly, pulling her from her thoughts. "You know, so I can see if there's any gleam in your eyes?"

She knew darn well there was a gleam in her eyes—it was practically burning her retinas. A gleam that matched the glitter simmering in his. And she also knew darn well that she wanted to see what would happen when those two gleams collided. See if this really was one of those Meant-to-Be Moments. Maybe she'd been all wrong about this guy. Only one way to find out...

Leaning across the small table, she settled her weight on her forearms and said, "Be my guest."

He reached out and slowly slid off her lenses. The tips of his fingers grazed her temples and she had to force herself not to lean into the feathery touch. The brim of her hat helped shade her eyes against the onslaught of bright sunlight, and after blinking twice, her gaze met his. And for several seconds she couldn't seem to breathe. Could only stare while her insides performed a crazy pirouette. Okay, sure the air was thin up here at eleven thousand feet, but this was *absurd.*

Appreciation, along with a flare of unmistakable

desire filled his eyes. "Wow," he murmured. "I was expecting pretty, but…wow." He cleared his throat. "In case you're wondering, 'wow' is a highly scientific term meaning 'you're gorgeous.'"

Her heart fluttered in the most ridiculously pleased way. "Thank you."

"Your eyes are the exact color of burning copper."

She blinked. "Uh, thanks. I think. But my eyes are green."

"Exactly. When copper is burned, it emits a green glow." His lips curved into a crooked, sheepish grin. "It's a whole laboratory, Bunsen-burner thing. Trust me…it's a compliment."

"In that case, thank you."

"You're welcome."

He handed her her sunglasses, and their fingers brushed, shooting a spark up her arm. In an effort to distract herself and keep from touching him to see if he'd cause another spark, she reached for her water. "So, what do you think I do for a living?"

"Magician," he answered without hesitation.

"And you guess that because…?"

He reached out and trailed a single fingertip over the back of her hand. "You've cast some sort of spell on me."

A sensual thrill zoomed through her, not only from his featherlight touch, but because he clearly felt this…whatever she was experiencing…too.

"Not a magician," she assured him.

"Victoria's Secret model?"

"Because you're hoping I am?"

"No, because you're beautiful enough to be one."

"Are you always such a flatterer?"

"No. In fact, I'm really bad at it—you've clearly already forgotten how I compared your eyes to burning copper. Something for which I should be grateful."

"Actually, I gave you points for originality."

"Oh? Good to know." His fingertip skimmed over her hand once again, then he leaned back in his chair and gave her a speculative look. She barely refrained from stretching out her hand toward him in a silent invitation to touch her again. "About your profession… given that you're friendly and have no difficulties talking to people, I'd guess you're in sales or marketing."

She laughed. "You went from underwear model to marketing?"

"All part of the scientific method. How about talk-show hostess?"

"You were closer with marketing. I'm in public relations."

He nodded. "Yes, that makes sense." His grin flashed. "So, what sort of relations do you have with the public?"

Not the sort I'm suddenly fantasizing about sharing with you. "Some good, some troublesome. Some clients are easy to deal with, others require more…finesse."

"I'm sure you're very good at it."

"I am," she said, without false modesty. Because she *was* good at her job, and she worked damned hard. "But lately…" Her voice trailed off and she frowned, wondering why she'd continued.

"But lately what?"

She shrugged, not prepared to confide feelings she barely understood herself to a man she scarcely knew, and also unwilling to say anything that might cast a pall on their easy camaraderie. Forcing a smile, she said lightly, "Lately I've needed a change. Which is why I'm here."

He raised his bottle of water. "Amen to that."

She tapped the rim of her drink against his and took a sip, watching him tip back his head to draw a long swallow, his strong throat working, his large hand dwarfing the bottle. Good grief, he even looked good when he drank water.

When he lowered his drink, their eyes met and held, and just as before, she felt the impact of his direct, compelling gaze like a heated wallop. One that made her breath catch, but not in any way she could blame on the eleven-thousand-foot altitude.

"Which hiking tour are you taking?" he asked.

"It's a four-day, three-night tour with Inca Trail Explorations. It departs at eight o'clock tomorrow morning." She shot him a half smile. "I'm not sure if I'm more excited or more nervous."

"Do you know your guide's name?"

"Not off the top of my head, but I can easily find out." She pulled the leather pouch where she kept all her travel documents from her tote bag, then scanned her tour itinerary. "His name is Paolo Trucero." She looked up from the papers. "I'm hoping Paolo's done this a thousand times before and knows what he's doing."

"According to my travel agent, he does." His lips curved into a sexy, lopsided smile. "I'm on that same tour."

She feigned surprise and experienced a sharp, unexpected jolt of self-reproach. A guilt-induced heated flush swept up her back all the way to her scalp, and she wished she'd slipped her sunglasses back on to hide her eyes to prevent him from possibly seeing the truth—that she knew damn well they were on the same tour. She wanted to look away from his warmly admiring regard which only served to heap on more guilt.

What had happened to her desire for payback? Darned if she knew. All she did know was that revenge was not among the tingly feelings this man inspired.

Would he guess the truth? Part of her almost wished he would so as to put an end to her spying mission which she found less and less palatable with each passing minute. But no hint of suspicion showed in his gaze. No, instead he was looking at her as if he'd just been given an unexpected gift. *Hello, another layer of guilt.*

She offered him a smile. "Looks like we'll be spending the next four days together."

"I'm thinking that's good news."

"I'm thinking I agree."

"Are you hungry?" he asked.

An image instantly materialized in her mind...of him and her, naked, sweaty, her legs wrapped around his waist, him thrusting deep inside her.

Heat pooled in her stomach and she had to swallow twice to find her voice, and even then only managed a whisper. "Starving."

"A porter at my hotel recommended a place at the other end of the plaza that serves everything from local dishes to wood-fire pizzas. He assured me the food is good and embarrassingly cheap. Would you care to join me?"

Another erotic image flashed through her mind...of her joining him under the deluge of a hot, steamy shower. She blinked to clear the image. No wonder it was recommended that travelers give themselves at least a day to get used to the altitude. The thin air was clearly affecting her ability to think of anything other than sex. Or maybe it was just that for the first time in a long time, she felt…free. With no one to look after except herself. No family drama to deal with. There was, of course, the work issue—the reason she was here—but spending time with Brett Thornton was precisely what she was supposed to be doing. Right?

Or maybe it was that she found herself not only extremely attracted to this man, but curious about him as well. Her instincts—which she considered very reliable—were telling her that this man was trustworthy, and not the sort to make false claims. And that if he blew off an important party, maybe he'd had a good reason for doing so. Still, she needed to consider that her instincts might be somewhat derailed by the surge of hormones racing through her body.

But, regardless of the reason, there was only one answer to his question. "I'd love to join you." She shot him a teasing grin. "But what if we share a meal together and discover we can't stand each other? It might make things awkward on the trail."

He rested his forearms on the table and leaned forward. His face was no more than a foot from hers and her breath caught at the heat simmering in his gaze. "Somehow I don't think that's going to be problem. But I'm willing to risk it if you are."

And again, there was only one answer. Looking into his eyes, she said, "I'm willing to risk it."

4

A WAITER ESCORTED them to a quiet, secluded alcove in the back room of the nearly deserted restaurant, ensconcing them in a privacy that felt both warm and intimate. Once seated amongst the richly colored Andean textiles and exposed Inca stonework, Brett pretended to study the menu, but in reality he was studying the woman seated adjacent to him.

She'd removed her straw hat, revealing a sleek, glossy cap of chin-length auburn hair that his fingers itched to touch. He was debating the wisdom of giving in to the urge when she raised her gaze from the menu. "Have you decided what you want?" she asked.

You. In so many ways it's making my head spin. "You mean from the menu?"

He really liked the heat that flared in her eyes. "Yes. For now."

And he also really liked that she wasn't shy. And that she clearly felt this same strong attraction as he. Setting down his menu, he said, "My Spanish consists mostly of silent gestures." He demonstrated by nodding yes, shaking his head, then mimed asking for the check. "How's yours?"

"Also pretty basic. I can say, 'Where's the hospital?' 'Where's the bathroom?' and 'I need a policeman.'"

"Clearly our priorities are different because my two basic phrases contain the words *cold beer* and *hot food*."

She laughed. "Between the two of us we have the necessities covered. You teach me your phrases and I'll teach you mine."

"I don't know. Yours are all about asking for directions, which is something men don't do. Do you know anything useful like—" he reached out and lightly entwined their fingers "—'My dinner companion has the softest hands I've ever felt?'"

Her breath caught at the contact, then her lips twitched. "I'm afraid not. But I do know that *pizza* means, well, pizza, and that *queso* and *tomate* mean cheese and tomato, so I think I can order us a decent meal without too much trouble."

"Excellent. I'll leave the dinner order in your capable hands. Knowing my luck, I'd end up ordering something like sautéed earthworms by mistake."

"I understand they serve those on the trail to Machu Picchu," she said with a teasing grin.

"Thanks for the warning."

She placed their order to the smiling waiter by pointing to the items on the menu she wanted. After he departed, Brett made an exaggerated eye roll and said, "Well, *I* could have done that."

"Uh-huh. And we'd have ended up with sautéed earthworms." She glanced down to where their fingers remained lightly joined, and he followed her gaze. Her hand looked remarkably small and pale and smooth next to his, and the sight of their entwined fingers looked stirringly intimate. And utterly arousing. His fingers bore dozens of pale scars from nicks and cuts and burns, mostly from childhood chemistry experiments. Luckily he'd gotten smarter and more coordinated as he'd grown. When he raised his gaze, he found her studying him.

"Care to share why your life's out of balance?" she asked in a light tone. "If you tell me, I'll tell you."

He leaned forward and gave in to his craving to touch her hair. It was as silky-soft as it looked. "Okay," he agreed, already deciding to offer up the very abridged version. "But you first."

Kayla pondered for a few seconds, then decided to give him the full story, hoping that if she were open with him, he'd reciprocate. Reaching with her free hand into her bag, she pulled out her *U.S. Weekly Review* then opened it to the *No Change, No Gain* article and pointed to the first paragraph.

"'Sex, love, career, family, friendships, marriage,'" she said, quoting the words. Then she looked at him. "Every one of those is, in some way, out of balance for me."

He raised his brows. "Please tell me you're not married."

"*I'm* not, but my older sister, Meg, is getting married next month and I'm the maid of honor. Have you ever heard the term *bridezilla?*"

"No, but it doesn't sound good—like a cross between a bride and Godzilla?"

"That's exactly what it is, and it's not good at all. This wedding has been in the planning stages for over a year, and to put it bluntly, it's a nightmare that has turned my already type-A sister into a crazy person. She's micromanaging every detail to death and driving everyone insane over the most ridiculous things—at least they seem ridiculous to me. I mean, does it really matter if the color of the cocktail napkins is eggshell instead of ecru?"

"Wouldn't seem so, but then, I wouldn't know eggshell from hot pink, so I'm not a good person to ask."

"She calls me constantly to talk about the flowers or the photographer or the caterer or her future in-laws or how Robert—that's her fiancé—isn't helping her." She shook her head. "They're both lawyers and could argue the paint off the walls. Personally, I think Robert's just tired of arguing, which is saying a lot."

"So you're saying I'm not missing much by being an only child."

She laughed. "I love both my sisters, but there are definitely days when I wish they'd lose my phone number."

He scooted his chair closer and lightly massaged her hand with both of his. "What's your other sister like?"

"Hmmm...that feels nice." Her eyes drifted closed. "Reeaally nice. What was the question?"

He chuckled and kept on massaging. "Your other sister."

"Oh, right. Cindy is the youngest. Last week she pulled off an incredible trifecta. She graduated from college, announced she was moving to Los Angeles with her actor boyfriend, Jason, who just scored a minor part in the James Bond flick about to start shooting, *and* that she's pregnant."

"That *is* quite a triple play."

"You have no idea. She's been calling every day to ask for baby advice, as if I have any. Although, I have to admit I'm pretty excited about being an aunt. Not so with Meg. The news sent the bride-to-be into hysterics because now not only is she afraid that Cindy won't fit into her Vera Wang bridesmaid dress, but she's upset that everyone will be talking about the pregnancy and Jason's movie role on *her* big day. She calls me hourly, alternately crying and complaining. I've taken to putting her on the speakerphone with the volume waaay down."

"You might do better to just unplug the phone."

"That's next. Then there's Mom. She can't decide if she's more distraught that Cindy is pregnant without, as she puts it, 'benefit of clergy,' or by the fact that she's going to be a grandmother, which she claims she's far too young to be. She calls several times a day to discuss either the wedding or the baby. When she isn't talking about one of those things, she's playing matchmaker, trying to set me up with every single man she can find." Kayla blew out a huff of laughter. "Between the three of them calling me constantly, it's like I'm caught in a Bermuda triangle of telephone agony."

"No offense, but it sounds like you're the only sane one in the family."

"Only on days when I don't answer my phone—which is becoming more and more frequent."

"Where does your father fit in?"

She paused for several seconds, then said, "He doesn't. He died five years ago."

"I'm sorry."

"Me, too. He was a great dad."

He nodded back toward the magazine. "Well, that explains about marriage and family."

"Friendships, too. Believe me, remaining friends with my family has been challenging lately."

"What about career?"

She hesitated, not certain how to explain without slipping up and giving away too much. "I've worked very hard to get where I am in my company, and I've always enjoyed my work. But lately, I've become...disenchanted with many of the people I'm working with. I've found them shallow and lacking in character." Again she hesitated, then added softly, "It's made me wonder if perhaps some of that hasn't rubbed off on me."

"You don't seem shallow to me."

"Says a man who's known me all of two hours."

His fingers lightly brushed over hers, the feathery touch pulsing heat up her arm. "True, but I'd be willing to bet that I'd say the same thing two hours from now." He studied her for several seconds, his expression serious. "But I know what you mean. When you find yourself surrounded by superficial people, it's easy to fall into that trap. To lose sight of yourself. And your goals."

She nodded, surprised that he'd hit it so precisely. "Yes. That's it exactly."

"But your strength of character shows in that you recognize yourself falling. And you're taking steps to change direction, to get back to where you want to be. You shouldn't be so hard on yourself for taking a slight detour."

"This sounds like the voice of experience talking."

A slight frown creased between his brows. "I guess it is." His thumbs brushed slowly over the backs of her hands, a hypnotic gesture that lulled her into a pleasure-filled trance. "So that leaves love and sex," he murmured. "Surely you have men begging for your company."

"You know, you're extremely good for my ego."

"Just calling it like I see it. Bad breakup?"

"You can't have a breakup unless you have a relationship, and my last one of those ended six months ago after I discovered we held polar opposite views regarding monogamy."

"What's your view?"

"At the point we were in our relationship, I felt it was essential. He was equally adamant it was optional. He claimed he loved me, but didn't love *only* me. I decided he could love as many women as he wanted—but I wasn't going to be one of them. Since then, my love life has consisted of a parade of really, really awful first dates." She shuddered. "If you strung them together, they'd be a bad movie entitled *Jerks, Egomaniacs, Cheaters and Other Assorted Whackos I've Recently Dated.*"

"How can a guy cheat after only one date?"

"He cheated *on* the date. With one of the waitresses. In the ladies' room. I recognized his shoes under the stall door. Based on the animal grunts, they were exchanging more than phone numbers."

He winced. "Ouch. That's really low. Makes me embarrassed to belong to the same gender as someone who would do that."

She forced her attention from the magic his long, strong fingers were wreaking on her hand and wondered if he was sincere. He certainly sounded as if he meant it. "Definitely ranks as one of my worst first dates."

"*This* first date is going very well," he said.

"Is this a date?" She found herself holding her breath, waiting for his answer.

"A nice restaurant, a cozy, private alcove all to ourselves, a beautiful woman…feels like a date to me."

Yes, it did. And she wasn't really certain how she felt about that. Certainly it was unexpected. As was his effect on her. The last time a man had made her feel like this…like she'd been struck by lightning, was…never.

"Well, this is definitely an improvement on the date with the guy who boffed the waitress in the bathroom," she said lightly.

"Thanks, but that isn't a high benchmark to exceed."

"True. But if you claim to need the restroom, I'll be mighty suspicious."

"Not to worry. You have my full and undivided attention. Where are you meeting these losers?"

"Losers? Oh, no, my friend. They're the best Manhattan has to offer."

"Present company excluded, I hope." He turned over her hand and traced his fingertip slowly around her palm, shooting fiery tingles up her arm and evaporating her concentration.

She had to swallow to find her voice. "Um, yeah. So far you're way ahead of the Bathroom Banger." And suddenly the thought of a hot, sweaty bang in the bathroom sounded really, really good. And far too tempting. And not her usual style. Certainly not with a man she'd just met.

Hey—it's not as if he's a complete stranger, her inner voice interjected.

Hmmm…very true. Even though they hadn't met, Brett Thornton had been on her radar screen for the past four months. She had an entire file on him, filled with scientific articles he'd written—the technical aspects of which had glazed her eyes—and information about his education and professional life, but little regarding his personal life. Up until now she hadn't cared to know.

But that was before she'd discovered that he could make her entire body flush hot with a single look. A single touch. It was definitely time to know more about this man whom she was envisioning naked—and liking what she saw. And to find out if her touch affected him as strongly as his did her.

"I've kept up my end of the bargain," she said, slipping her hand from beneath his. "Now it's your turn. What in your life is out of balance?"

Brett carefully considered before answering, surprised by his strong urge to tell her the entire story. He'd come all the way to freakin' Peru to partake in an extreme adventure, one he hoped would exorcise the poison of the last few months. He sure as hell hadn't come here thinking he'd be anxious to talk to a stranger about what a mess his life had become. Then again, he hadn't thought he'd be anxious to begin an affair, most especially not with just the sort of woman he'd sworn to himself to avoid—one who had Fifth Avenue written all over her—but here he was, hot, bothered and aching.

He was about to speak when she settled her hand on his leg, just above his knee. His heart ricocheted for a few beats, pumping heat through him. When she'd said it was "his turn," she'd obviously meant in more ways than one.

After taking a long swallow of water, he looked pointedly down at where her palm rested on his bare knee then said, "God knows I'm game, but I feel it only fair to warn you that I'm not sure how long I'll be able to remain focused."

Mischief danced in her eyes and her fingertips skimmed down his shin. "Turnabout is only fair."

"I only touched your hand. So you'll owe me."

Her eyes darkened in a way that let him know she wasn't averse to paying up, and what felt like half the blood in his body rushed to his groin. He shifted to relieve the ache and stretched out his leg to offer her freer access. And hoped he wouldn't forget how to speak English.

"Ever hear of that expression 'be careful what you wish for because you may just get it?'" he asked.

She smiled and circled her fingertips behind his knee. Holy crap. She'd barely touched him and he felt as if he were about to spontaneously combust. "Of course," she said in a smoky voice. "I'm hoping it will apply to me and winning the lottery."

With an effort, he shook his head. "Just trust me…you don't want to say those words out loud."

"Hmmm…I've found that when people say 'just trust me' I probably shouldn't. Are you saying you won the lottery and that it sucks—'cause I'd have a hard time believing that."

A hard time…thanks to her slowly roaming fingers, he knew all about a hard time. "Not the lottery. But after years of research, I reached a personal and professional goal. Sort of a scientific breakthrough."

"That sounds like a good thing."

"I agree. But I found out very quickly that a lot of bad stuff came with the good."

Understanding dawned in her eyes—which he nearly missed because her fingertips brushed beneath the hem of his khaki shorts, glazing his eyes over. "Everyone suddenly wanted in on *your* breakthrough," she said, and he thanked God his hearing was still operating. "Professional jealousy and all that."

"Um, something like that, yes. And, like the person

who wins the lottery, I suddenly found myself with lots and lots of 'friends.'"

Her eyes twinkled. "Ah-ha. So you *did* win the lottery. Are you sure I won't try to hit you up for a loan?"

"If you keep touching my leg like that, I'm apt to give you anything you want."

Her fingers slid a bit higher on his leg and he sucked in a breath. "Good to know," she murmured, drawing slow, drugging circles around his inner thigh.

"But to set the record straight, I didn't win the lottery, and you'd be sorely disappointed in my bank balance."

"So then these false friends are trying to ride your professional coattails and share in your glory?"

He nodded even though it was only half of the problem, the other part being the relentless pursuit by the cosmetics companies, but her touch was rapidly depleting his ability to prolong the conversation. "I felt as if I was being pulled in a dozen directions, and I was losing sight of what was important. Of who I was and what I wanted. I needed to get away. *Far* away. Clear my head."

"No change, no gain."

"Exactly."

"So what other aspects of your life were out of balance?" she asked.

"Family and friendships are fine, and since I'm not married, that's not an issue."

"What about love and sex?"

"I'm completely unattached."

Deciding two could play at this game, he leaned forward and reached beneath the table to lightly grasp her ankle, enjoying her quick intake of breath. "And one of the first people I meet is from the same city I just flew nearly four thousand miles to escape. Unbelievable."

"Sorry. If I'd known you were trying to escape all reminders of home, I wouldn't have said hello."

He stroked his fingers up her silky calf, a move she answered by stroking her palm higher up his thigh. "If you hadn't said hello that would have been my very great loss."

"Maybe not. I think I probably would have said hello anyway."

"Why's that?"

"Fishing for compliments?"

He slipped his hand over her knee. "Shamefully."

Her gaze roamed his face, then said softly, "Something about the way you were sitting there, your expression. You looked..." She shook her head. "I'm not sure how to describe it other than to say that you looked how I felt. Glad to be here, yet somehow...lonely."

He studied her eyes and his stomach seemed to swoop downward, as if he were falling. Which, crazy as it sounded, was precisely how he felt—as if he was in an emotional free fall. He'd gone from zero to lust to halfway in love with this woman in a millisecond.

"I was lonely," he said, softly stroking her knee, "although I hadn't even realized it. But I'm not anymore."

"I'm glad. But I would have said hello to you anyway because I also thought you were really cute."

"Right back at ya. Except I don't think *cute* really does you justice."

"Oh? What would you say does?"

"Fishing for compliments?"

"Shamefully."

After considering for several seconds, he said, "You possess an abundance of millihelens and microhelens."

"Whatever that means."

"You've heard of Helen of Troy?"

"The woman over whom the Trojan War was started?"

"That's the one. It's said that her face launched a thousand ships. In the Troy system of units, a millihelen is the amount of beauty required to launch *one* ship. A microhelen is roughly the amount of beauty needed to motivate one sailor." His fingertips skimmed behind her knee. "You possess enough of both to launch an entire armada of ships and motivate an entire army of soldiers."

A slow, sexy smile curved her lips. She tickled her fingertips across his thigh and he damn near forgot how to breathe. "Thank you. Looks like I'll be giving you some more points for originality."

"Excellent. How can I earn a few more?"

"You could dazzle me with some interesting scientific facts."

"One square inch of skin contains six hundred and twenty-five sweat glands." He edged his hand higher under her skirt and slowly traced his fingers up her thigh. He noted with satisfaction that her own fingers stilled on his leg and her pupils dilated when his fingers drew leisurely figure eights on her exquisitely soft skin.

"I believe it," she murmured in a breathless voice. "I feel like every one of mine is pumping steam."

Without taking his gaze from hers, he rose, then gently pulled her to her feet. Hidden in their private alcove in the back room, he drew her into his arms and slowly skimmed his hands down her back. "In the adult human body, there are forty-six miles of nerves. The most sensitive cluster of nerves is here..." He lightly massaged the small of her back, urging her closer, until their bodies touched from chest to knee. "At the base of the spine."

"Fascinating," she murmured, skimming her hands up his chest then looping her arms around his neck. "What else?"

"Minks have sex that lasts about eight hours."

"Oh...my."

"Moose intercourse usually lasts about five seconds."

"Note to self...would much prefer to be a mink."

Leaning forward, he nuzzled the warm, smooth skin just below her ear with his lips. God, she smelled delicious.

"Bats have sex in the air."

She breathed out a sigh then tilted her neck, affording him better access. "Sounds...adventurous."

His teeth lightly nipped her earlobe. "A female praying mantis devours her partner while they're mating."

"Mmm. Depending on your definition of *devour,* that could also sound adventurous."

"A female ferret can die if she goes into heat and can't find a mate."

Her fingers fisted in his hair and with a groan, she tugged his mouth towards her. "I know exactly how she feels," she said in a husky whisper against his lips.

His mouth covered hers in kiss that drained every thought from his head. He'd intended to kiss her gently, seduce her slowly, savoring each touch, but the instant their lips met, a flash-fire reaction the likes of which he'd never before experienced sizzled through him, incinerating him where he stood.

She tasted as seductively delicious as she smelled, and, with a low growl, his arms tightened around her. He stepped backwards until his shoulders hit the wall, then he spread his legs, settling her in the V of his thighs, pressing her tighter against his erection, and feasted on her lush mouth, while his hands roamed restlessly up and down her back.

His tongue mated with hers, an erotic friction that quickly depleted whatever control she hadn't already stolen. His hands skimmed over her lush curves, settling on her bottom. She shifted against him, dragging another growl from his throat. His hips involuntarily thrust into her feminine softness, and he knew they needed to stop this *now*...before he stood in real danger of not being able to stop at all.

Expending an effort that required all his will power, he lifted his head. Breathing hard, he looked down into her flushed face. Her hair was beautifully messed from his impatient hands, and with her lips parted and moist from their frantic kiss and her eyelids droopy, she looked sinfully aroused and sexy as hell.

Her tongue peeked between her lips, a flick of pink that spiked his temperature another few degrees. She blinked twice, a look of utter confusion filling her glazed eyes. "What *was* that?"

He shook his head, feeling as bemused and jumbled as she looked. "Damned if I know."

"I...I'm at a loss to explain being so carried away."

"Scientifically, I'd describe it as an instantaneous exothermic reaction."

"Which means what, to those of us whose brain cells seem to have melted?"

"Basically, it's a very fast, strong reaction that gives off heat—like when firecrackers explode."

"Yes, that explains it very well. Although I'd have just called it 'magic.'"

"Magic works for me."

"Exactly what sort of science is your specialty that you know all this?"

He tucked a stray strand of shiny auburn hair behind her ear. "Chemistry. The study of matter and the changes that it undergoes…or what's happening between us."

"Can't argue with that."

"I don't suppose you know how to say 'Can we get our meal to go?' in Spanish?"

"No, but *adios* means goodbye. Probably if we said that, the waiter would get the point."

"I'm willing to give it a try." His hands lightly kneaded her bottom and every reason why he didn't have the time or inclination for a relationship melted under the onslaught of heat between them. *Relationship?* his inner voice scoffed. *No problem—this is just sex.* Part of his mind instantly disagreed, but he ignored the warning.

Swallowing a moan of raw want, he said, "We either need to stop this or get out of here now. I know which one gets my vote. How about you?"

She looked at him with those beautiful green eyes smoldering with arousal, with the same wild need racing through him, and his heart performed a crazy rollover maneuver.

"Let's get out of here," she said. "Now."

5

WALKING ACROSS the Plaza de Armas, her fingers entwined with Brett's, Kayla drew several deep breaths and waited for her sanity to return. For her common sense to override her screaming libido. For her better judgment to cough to life and tell her that going to the hotel room of a man she barely knew wasn't a good idea.

But instead of any of that, her heart simply whispered, *I know enough for now. And I want to know more.*

Never had she experienced such a wild, instant attraction. Or felt so carried away, so unable to think beyond the desperate need to get naked with a man. It was a fiery, heady, impossible-to-ignore sensation she couldn't deny herself the pleasure of seeing through to the end.

Still, she felt compelled to say, "Brett, I want you to know…I don't normally do this."

He slowed his pace and turned to look at her. "This?"

"One-night stands. With someone I just met."

He halted, set down the bag containing their boxed pizza, then framed her face between his hands. Serious golden-brown eyes studied hers for several long seconds. She wanted him to voice the words swimming through her mind—that somehow this didn't feel like a one-night stand. That it felt intense, and unsettling because of that intensity. Instead he asked softly, "Did we just meet?"

Her throat went dry and for a panicked instant she wondered if he'd seen her at La Fleur. Before she could even think of a plausible reply, he continued, "Because it doesn't feel like it, Kayla. As crazy as it sounds, I feel as if I know you. As if I *have* known you. For a long time." A humorless sound escaped him and what looked like confusion passed over his features. "It's illogical and unscientific, but…"

"Undeniable?"

He nodded, still regarding her as if she were a puzzle he was trying to solve. "I know chemistry when I see it. Hell, I know it when I feel it. But at the risk of sounding like I'm tossing out a line from some love song, I've never felt it like this before."

"Thank God it's not just me." She settled her hands on his chest. "Maybe it's the altitude."

"Maybe. But I think it's my molecules just really, really liking your molecules."

She smiled. "How lucky for my molecules."

"And mine. And if it makes you feel any better, one-night stands aren't my usual thing either. Besides, since we're on the same tour, this might turn into a two- or three- or even four-night stand." He brushed his thumbs over her cheeks. "Any more second thoughts?"

Kayla looked into his eyes and a tremor of pure want shook her. She'd come to Cusco because of Dr. Thornton, but she was here, wrapped in these strong arms because of Brett. Being with him, like this, had nothing to do with La Fleur and everything to do with her. And him. And how much they wanted each other. Making love with him would be the first thing she'd done just for herself in a long time. Indeed, it didn't matter where she might have met this man—here, New York, Timbuktu—she would have made love with him. The chemistry between them was just too strong to ignore.

"If I had any other second thoughts," she said, "the fact that you're making my knees shake by just *looking* at me kinda shoves them to the background."

He brushed his lips over hers, stopping her breath. "To repeat your phrase, thank God it's not just me."

Her fingers curled, clutching his shirt. "Do you have condoms?" she asked, praying he did.

"Yeah," he whispered against her lips. "Anything else you want to know?"

"Yeah. How fast can we get to your room?"

After a brief, pulse-quickening kiss, he snatched up the pizza then grabbed her hand. "Let's find out."

They started off at a brisk walk which turned into a jog. By the time they neared the small hotel, Kayla was breathless with a combination of anticipation, laughter and exertion from the high altitude.

"I think I've exhausted myself," she gasped, climbing the last two steps to the second floor. When she reached the top, he handed her the pizza, swung her up in his arms and strode swiftly down the hallway.

"Don't worry," he said. "I have enough energy for both of us."

Kayla wrapped an arm around his neck then leaned forward to nibble his earlobe. "I didn't know scientists were so strong."

"Obviously you've been hanging out with biologists.

Or physicists. Bunch of weaklings those guys are. Now chemists—we know how to build muscles."

"Obviously," she murmured, running an appreciative hand over his wide, solid chest. "Probably I'll get a second wind."

"If not, I'll do my best to revive you."

"You know CPR?"

He shot her a wink. "Sweetheart, I know all sorts of ways to jump-start your heart."

Her pulse quivered at the mere thought. "Lucky me."

He stopped in front of the last door. "Hang on," he said, letting go with the hand that was wrapped around her waist. "Gotta find the key."

"You could put me down," she suggested, her lips continuing their exploration of his jaw.

"Not a chance. I'm not letting go. Do you know why men carry women over thresholds?"

"No clue. But I bet a genius boy like you does."

"It's to protect them from being possessed by the evil spirits that hang around in doorways."

"And here I thought it was just an amazingly romantic gesture."

"That, too." She gently bit his neck and he groaned. "You know, you're not making the key search any easier."

"Good. I want it hard."

"Sweetheart, if it gets any harder—" His words ended on a strangled sound and she heard the metallic jangle of a key. The door swung open and he stepped inside, pushing it firmly closed with his foot. Then he set her down.

The instant her feet touched the floor, Kayla dropped her canvas tote and the pizza box. His eyes glittered with so much sensual heat, even the soles of her feet felt hot.

"If it gets any harder...what?" she asked, leaning against the wall, her gaze flicking pointedly down at the impressive bulge in his shorts.

He reached out and locked the door. "It can't. Get any harder. Impossible." With each choppy sentence, he moved closer, until he stood directly in front of her, then braced his hands on the wall, caging her in. Mere inches separated them and she could feel the heat emanating from him. Smell his skin, warm, clean and musky, mixed with the subtle fresh scent of his soap. His eyes, intense and darkened with arousal, met hers, and fiery tingles shivered to her every nerve ending.

"Oh, I bet it can get harder." Reaching out, she pressed her palm against his erection. He sucked in a breath, then released it in a long groan as she gently squeezed him.

"I won't last long if you keep doing that," he said, lightly grasping her wrist.

"That's fine by me," she said, pushing the words past her dry throat. God help her, she couldn't ever recall feeling this desperate. She was practically panting and could barely speak. "I'm not going to last long myself."

"Yeah? Let's see." In one swift move, he clasped her waist and turned them so that he now leaned against the wall. Before she could draw a deep breath, his mouth covered hers, and the magic he'd wrought in the restaurant began all over again.

Only this was...more. Deeper. Fiercer. Hotter. More passionate. And now there was nothing to stop them. Impatience raced through her, her entire body humming with anticipation. Desperate to touch him, she yanked his T-shirt from his waistband and plunged her hands beneath the soft material.

Warm…his skin was so warm. And smooth. Her palms coasted over rippled abs, tracing the fine ribbon of hair that bisected his rock-hard torso. Her hands skimmed higher, her splayed fingers sifting through soft, crisp curls. She pushed his shirt upward, but her efforts were distracted as his hands were suddenly…everywhere. Pulling down her stretchy tank top to expose her breasts. The clever fingers of one hand arousing her already hard nipples, while the other glided under her skirt. Hooking beneath her knee and raising her leg to his waist, opening her to his touch.

His fingers slipped beneath her wisp of lacy panties and she groaned at his first exquisite touch of her sex. He broke off their kiss and trailed his tongue down her neck as he caressed her swollen folds with a skill that made her knees go weak.

"You're so wet," he murmured against her skin. "So silky and hot."

"All your fault…ahhh…" Her words trailed off in a long sigh when he slipped two fingers inside her. Unable to stop herself she undulated against his hand, greedily absorbing the quickening, deep strokes. His palm pressed against her with just the right pressure and her climax roared through her, a series of deep, shuddering spasms that dragged a cry from her throat. She clung to his shoulders, absorbing the aftershocks, her ragged breaths burning her lungs.

When Kayla could manage it, she dragged open her eyes. And found him watching her with an expression that would have melted her if he hadn't already managed to do so.

She licked her lips to moisten them, then whispered,

"Told you I wouldn't last long. Thank you—for putting out that damn fire you started."

His lips twitched. "My pleasure."

"Not as much as it was mine, believe me. But I'll make sure I even the score."

He leaned forward and brushed his mouth over hers. "Looking forward to that."

"And I'll get right on it. As soon as you give me back my knees. Seems I took one look at you and they fell off."

He chuckled then dipped down and scooped her up in his arms. "So I guess you'd better lie down," he said, striding toward the bed. "That's a real shame—having a gorgeous woman sprawled in my bed. A damn hardship, but I'll try to grin and bear it." He plopped her down on the center of the multicolored bedspread where she landed with a gentle bounce. "Don't go away," he said, then turned toward the closet.

"As if you'd get rid of me." She watched him dig through a dark blue backpack, presumably for condoms. Her body was already tingling at the prospect of another round—this time with their clothes off. In anticipation of his return, she kicked off her sandals, then shimmied out of her tank top, skirt and panties. Stretching out on the bed, a slow smile curved her lips.

Time to get this party started.

6

BRETT RIFLED through his backpack, trying to stave off the impatience clawing at him. Where the hell were the damn condoms? And why did this damn bag have so many damn compartments? He yanked on another zipper, and relief filled him at the sight of the familiar packets. He'd slipped them in out of habit, not because he'd thought he'd actually need them. He grabbed one then stood and turned toward the bed. And froze. And stared.

At Kayla, who reclined on his bed, her head propped against the pillows. At Kayla, whose shiny auburn hair was beautifully mussed from his hands and whose skin was kissed by a fascinating splash of pale freckles and painted gold by the rays of late-afternoon sun slanting through the window. And who wore nothing save a wicked smile.

His gaze tracked down her body, over full breasts topped with coral nipples, generous hips, long, shapely legs…she was curvy and luscious and sinful and holy hell, just looking at her rushed more blood to his groin.

Talk about an instantaneous reaction.

He forced several slow, careful breaths into his lungs, then walked toward her. When he neared the bed, he tossed the condom onto the nightstand, and was about to remove his shirt when she shook her head and rolled onto her knees.

"Allow me." Reaching out, she slid his Hawaiian print shirt off his shoulders and dropped it at his feet. "All you have to do is relax," she said, slipping her hand beneath his T-shirt.

"Relax?" He huffed out a laugh that turned into a groan when her hands skated up his torso. "You can't be serious."

She pushed up his T-shirt, and he raised his arms so she could pull it over his head. Seconds later it joined his Hawaiian shirt on the floor."

"Then just stay still," she murmured, slowly dragging her hands down his chest.

"Gotta tell ya, that's asking a *lot...*" The last word ended on a groan when she leaned forward and pressed her lips to the center of his chest.

"Maybe," she whispered, her warm breath breezing over his skin, "but you will be rewarded for your compliance." Leaning back, she flicked her gaze down to his feet. "Footwear off."

While he toed off his sneakers then removed his socks, he said in the most teasing tone he could muster, considering his straining erection, "First it's 'relax,' then 'remain still,' now 'footwear off'...has anyone ever told you that you're kinda bossy?"

"I prefer to think of it as being a take-charge sort of gal. One who's not afraid to say what she wants. And right now I want you to stand still while I get you naked so I can repay you for that fabulous orgasm you just gave me." She hooked a single fingertip into the waistband of his shorts and yanked him closer. "Any complaints?"

"Hell, no. I like a woman who's upfront. But before we begin," he reached out and cupped her full breasts, his fingers gently tugging at her nipples, enjoying her low moan of pleasure, "just so you know, I'm not afraid to say what I want, either. And I'll want to see your orgasm and raise you two more."

"Oooh, sounds like orgasm poker," she crooned in a sultry voice.

"That's exactly what it is. Wanna play?"

"By all means. Let the games begin."

Her eyes gleaming with heated mischief, she gently grasped his wrists, settled his hands at his sides, then flicked open the button of his shorts.

Brett stood in an agony of anticipation, watching her slowly lower his zipper then slip her hands inside his waistband to push his boxers and shorts down in a single, fluid motion. When the clothes hit his ankles, he stepped out of them and pushed them aside with his foot, heaving a massive sigh of relief that his body no longer felt strangled.

But his relief was short-lived as she pressed her palms against his chest and urged him back several paces. Then she moved off the bed to stand before him, her avid gaze roaming over him.

"Very nice," she said, her fingertips drawing slow circles on his abdomen. His muscles jumped beneath her touch and he clenched his hands to keep from simply snatching her against him and devouring her.

"Glad you approve," he managed to say, his voice sounding as if he'd swallowed gravel.

Her gaze settled on his erection and she licked her lips. Fire raced through him, feeling that look, that lick, as if she'd actually touched him. Tasted him. His entire body tightened, and he seriously doubted his ability to remain still much longer.

And she hadn't even touched him yet.

God help him.

"Oh, I definitely approve," she said in a low, seductive voice he could only describe as a purr, one which didn't bode well for his rapidly evaporating control. She walked slowly around him, dragging her fingertips across his bare hip, until she stood directly behind him. "Rear view is...lovely. Tell me, is this the spot—" her fingers lightly circled the base of his spine "—where you said the most sensitive cluster of nerves in the body is located?"

He sucked in a breath. "Yeah. That's the spot."

Her fingers tickled over the area again, shooting arrows of pleasure through him. "Are you sure?" she asked, sounding puzzled. "Right here? Because I would have thought other places were more sensitive. I think perhaps we should conduct an experiment to test the validity of your assertion."

"Wow. I love it when you talk science to me."

"You're up for an experiment?"

He gazed pointedly down at his straining erection then looked at her over his shoulder. "Clearly."

A devilish gleam burned in her eyes. "Excellent. For each place I touch your body, I want you to give a number from one to ten, with ten being the most sensitive, and we'll see which spot wins. How does that sound?"

Like sweet torture. "Seeing as how I'm a man who appreciates a finely crafted experiment, it sounds really, really good."

"Really, really good...is that one of those highly scientific terms? Like 'wow'?"

"Yes. Except in this case, it's an understatement. Of gargantuan proportions."

"I see." Her fingers circled the back of his spine once again and a low moan escaped him. "Well?" she asked, pressing warm kisses across his shoulders. "What's your rating?"

"I give it a ten."

Her fingers dragged slowly downward, over his buttocks. "And this?"

"A ten."

She stepped closer to him, and he felt the warmth of her body down the entire length of his. Her hard nipples brushed his back, erotically teasing, and her fingers dipped lower to caress the backs of his thighs. "Here?"

"Ten," he said, his voice low and rough.

Kayla chuckled, the puff of breath caressing his overheated skin. "I'm seeing a pattern here."

"I'm *feeling* one."

She walked around to stand in front of him. Grasping his wrists, she raised his hands. "Behind your neck," she instructed. After he'd clasped his fingers together, she skimmed her talented fingertips down the undersides of his upraised arms. Heat shot to his every nerve ending. When she raised a questioning brow, he promptly decreed, "Ten."

Next she lightly circled his nipples. "Well?"

"Ten."

Leaning forward she dragged her wet tongue across his nipple then gently suckled.

He pulled in a breath. "Eleven."

Triumph flared in her eyes. “Ah-ha! A breakthrough. It appears not only that the spine might not be the most sensitive spot, but also that sensitivity depends not only on where you touch, but what you touch with—your fingers or your mouth.”

“You definitely could be on to something,” he agreed. “Further investigation is absolutely called for.”

“You don’t mind?”

“I’ll try to grin and bear it. For the sake of science.”

“That’s what I like—a team player.”

“I’m definitely game.”

Her fingertips skimmed lower to feather over his hips. He gripped his hands tighter together behind his neck as his muscles contracted in rolling spasms of pleasure.

“Ten,” he said.

Brett watched her hands coast over his thighs, down his legs, behind his knees, each time saying “Ten,” each pass of her hands further tightening his body and peeling away another layer of his control. Everywhere she touched him, it felt as if fire raced beneath his skin. And she’d touched him everywhere—except his penis, which strained upward, hard and aching. His breathing turned labored and the effort he expended to remain still had him nearly shaking. He didn’t know how much more of this he could take.

“Spread your legs,” she said.

His gaze snapped to hers, and without a word, he did as she asked. Her fingers dipped into the crease between his thighs and a low growl escaped him. With his gaze pinned to hers, he said in a rough voice, “Twelve.”

Her warm palm cupped his tight sac and gently squeezed. He sucked in a hard breath. “Fourteen.”

She released him, then trailed a single fingertip down his hard length. His erection jerked at the featherlight contact and he groaned. When he didn't speak, she asked, "Your rating?"

"Do it again."

After she obliged, he rasped, "Twenty."

She raised her brows. "Interesting." Her gaze rested on his arousal, and he tensed in expectation. When she wrapped her fingers around him, his eyes slammed shut and he pulled in a quick, harsh breath.

"Number?" she asked, gently squeezing him.

"Thirty." The word came out in a low groan and he opened his eyes. "And just FYI—my powers of speech are rapidly vanishing."

"Good. Let's see what this does." She sat on the edge of the bed, urged him closer, then leaned forward and gave his shaft a long, slow lick, from base to tip.

A tremor ran through him, but before he could recover, she licked him again, this time sweeping her tongue over the sensitive head before looking up at him through glittering green eyes.

"Well?" she asked.

"You're driving me insane."

She lazily circled the tip of her tongue around the engorged head and he clenched his teeth against the aching pleasure. "Good insane, or bad insane?"

"Good," he gasped, as she leaned forward and slowly drew him into her mouth. "So…ahhh…good."

He watched her draw him in deeper, and he lowered his hands to sift them unsteadily through her soft hair. The erotic sight and incredible feel of her hot, silky mouth moving over him with a slow, mind-destroying rhythm, the sensation of her hands dipping between his legs to cup and caress him, was quickly bringing him to the brink. His vision blurred when she engulfed him deeper and sucked. Hard. He held off coming by sheer will, but when she repeated that tight, control-shredding draw, he knew he was done.

With a feral groan, he eased himself free of her plump lips. She looked up at him with a heated expression that all but incinerated him where he stood.

"I haven't evened the score yet," she said.

"Believe me, it's about to be evened. But when it is, I want you with me."

He urged her back on the mattress, and grabbed the condom. After quickly rolling on the protection, he settled himself in the warm cradle of her spread thighs. Their eyes met as he slowly sank into her tight, wet heat.

"God...you feel—" he ground out.

"So incredibly good..." she whispered.

"So incredibly good," he agreed, sinking deeper.

Buried to the hilt, he briefly closed his eyes, absorbing the incredible sensation of her body clamped around him like a hot, silken fist. Then, with his gaze on hers, he eased out nearly all the way, and thrust deep. Her lips parted, emitting a low rumbling sound of approval. He thrust again and again, long, smooth, deep strokes that quickened into driving plunges, each one urging him closer to detonation. Her breathing turned choppy and her fingers bit into his shoulders. When a cry broke from her lips and she arched beneath him, Brett let himself go. His climax roared through his system, shudders racking him with hot jolts of pleasure. When the spasms subsided, he collapsed, burying his face in the warm, fragrant curve of her neck and fought to catch his breath.

He wasn't sure how much time passed before he mustered the strength to lift his head. When he did, his heart quickened at the sight of her.

With her skin flushed, hair in wild disarray, moist lips parted and kiss-swollen, Kayla looked completely sated. And utterly beautiful. Propping his weight on his forearms, he brushed a damp auburn strand from her rosy cheek. A low *hmmm* sounded in her throat and her eyelids fluttered open. Their gazes locked and he stilled, struck by a sensation of…something. Something he couldn't name because he'd never felt it before. But whatever it was, it was intense and warm and intimate, and while half of him liked it—a lot—its very intensity scared the crap out of the other half of him.

Forcing a lightness into his voice—one he really had to reach for—he said, "You look…deliciously dazed."

She stretched beneath him and smiled. "I *feel* deliciously dazed. And very smug. It would seem I shot your theory all to hell. Indeed, I think the final tally was, Spine—ten. Penis—was it thirty or forty?"

"More like thirty thousand. But you changed the entire hypothesis by using your mouth."

"Is that a complaint?"

"Hell, no. In fact, I can't wait to run my own experiment on you. See if I find similar results, or if it's just a guy thing. I vote for a nice, warm shower, then another round of orgasm poker. How does that sound?"

Her lips curved into a beautiful smile that stole his breath. "Deal me in, baby. Deal me in."

7

WEARING Brett's Hawaiian shirt, which covered her to midthigh, Kayla stepped onto the small balcony of his hotel room. Echoes of music and an indistinguishable hum of voices floated over the cool night air from the nearby Plaza de Armas which was lined with numerous lively bars and discos. The moon shone in the sky, a luminous pearl against black satin. Stars twinkled like handfuls of scattered diamonds, the perfect backdrop for the grandeur of the Andes visible in their silvery glow. A breeze ruffled her hair, bringing with it the savory scent of food, and her stomach rumbled. They'd polished off the pizza hours ago.

Settling herself on the wrought-iron chair, she rifled through her canvas bag for her cell phone. She wasn't sure how long Brett would be gone on his errand to hunt up some bottled water and snacks—what kind of hotel didn't offer room service anyway?—and since it appeared that she was spending the night here, she needed to grab what would probably be her only chance to privately check her messages.

Flipping open her phone, which she'd set on Silent, Kayla noted she had eight voice mails and twenty text messages in her inbox. With a sigh, she opted to get the voice mails over with first. Three of the messages were from Meg regarding the wedding plans—no big surprise there. Two from Cindy, one asking how she liked the name Butterfly for a girl, the other complaining about Meg. Two calls were from her mom, one reiterating she was too young to be a grandmother, the other reporting that her hairdresser's son's divorce was final and that he'd be *perfect* for Kayla and should she set up a date?

The last message was from Nelson, left an hour ago, and she stilled as she heard his voice coming through the phone. "Hope the reason you're not answering this call is because you're somewhere with Thornton finding out everything you can about him and that damn formula. Keep me informed."

She disconnected from voice mail and buried her face in her hands. Guilt weighed heavily on her, along with something else…something she was reluctant to name because she didn't like it. Didn't like the way it made her feel about herself and what she was doing. *Shame, perhaps?* her inner voice archly asked.

She blew out a long sigh. Yes, damn it, she was ashamed. Because she'd searched through his belongings as soon as he'd departed the room. Searched for something, anything that might offer the sort of clue Nelson expected her to find. But instead of feeling as if she were doing her job, she'd felt like a sneak. And she'd been disgusted with herself for invading his privacy. She'd had to force herself to do it, but that did little to assuage her conscience as she'd still done it. Her search had only served to tarnish the thrill and excitement of being with him with the crushing feeling that she no longer deserved to share such intimacies with him.

As soon as she'd discerned that he didn't carry any folders marked Secret Formula or notebooks with scientific notations, she'd ceased her search, but the damage to her conscience was done. All she'd learned was that he packed light, had an obvious liking for Hawaiian print shirts, and clearly didn't wear cologne. And that she didn't like herself very much at that moment.

Since not liking herself felt uncomfortably close to the truth, Kayla shoved the notion aside and concentrated on the only slightly less palatable feeling crushing her—guilt. Guilt which was impossible to ignore as it was bombarding her from two directions.

One direction hinged on the fact that during the six hours she'd spent in Brett's hotel room, she hadn't *once* thought about La Fleur or the formula or Nelson or her reason for being here. The spying. The payback for the embarrassment and anger Brett's rude departure from the La Fleur party had caused her with the board of directors. The bonus, perks and promotion Nelson had dangled before her like a diamond-encrusted carrot.

No, instead she'd thought of nothing but Brett. Of the incredible way he made her feel. How much she enjoyed his company. His intelligence and wit. His smile. His talented hands and mouth on her body. The single-minded concentration with which he explored and touched her.

His effect on her, her body and her senses, was nothing short of extraordinary. She'd experienced arousal and desire, lust and infatuation before, but this was like all those emotions tossed into a windstorm, then multiplied by ten. Which was ridiculous, considering she'd just met him. Yet her fierce attraction to him was undeniable.

Nor was it solely physical. Through the course of the afternoon and evening, she'd learned a great deal about him—all of which only served to confirm the favorable impression she'd formed when she'd first encountered him in the plaza.

Unfortunately the things she'd found out about him were not the sort of things Nelson wanted to know. He wanted to know if the formula really produced the anti-aging and aphrodisiac-like results Brett claimed, how it was able to do so, and what La Fleur needed to do to obtain it. Instead she'd discovered that Brett had played on his high-school tennis team. That he enjoyed a mean game of chess and singing in the shower, but he was completely tone-deaf and couldn't carry a tune if you handed it to him in a gift box, which had led to much laughter...which had led to much kissing, which had led to the discovery that singing was only thing he didn't excel at in the shower.

After their shower, while gorging on their pizza, she'd learned he'd been raised on Long Island, his parents still lived in the house where he grew up, he loved animals and museums, and disliked lima beans and noisy, trendy clubs. He always worked the *New York Times* crossword puzzle in ink, and his two closest friends were guys he'd known since grade school.

They'd discussed a wide array of topics, from movies—he liked old war films and new action-adventure flicks, anything where stuff was blown up, while she preferred romantic comedies—to books, where they'd discovered a mutual love of Agatha Christie and Harry Potter. They'd voted for the same candidate in the last election, and both loved Chinese food—although he preferred chicken with black bean sauce while her favorite was shrimp with broccoli. She liked attending the ballet while he preferred not attending the ballet *ever,* but they both enjoyed seeing Broadway shows.

She'd learned he was witty, intelligent and looked oh, so fine sitting cross-legged on a bedspread wearing nothing except a towel around his hips and a wicked gleam in his eyes. Never once had he bragged about what she knew from her file on him were his impressive professional credentials and affiliations. Nor had he mentioned his work, except to relate a couple of amusing laboratory disaster anecdotes.

She also knew he kissed better than any man she'd ever before kissed, that he was a skilled and generous lover, and that over the course of the evening, he'd brought her to orgasm *six* times. An image of them on the bed, the empty pizza box pushed to the floor along with their towels, her legs splayed wide and Brett's dark head between her thighs, flashed through her mind, and she waved her hand in front of her face to dispel the heat that whooshed through her.

The man had magic hands, magic lips, a magic tongue. Magic...everything. And she fully expected that after he returned with food and drinks and they'd refueled, another orgasm or two lurked in their immediate future. Certainly she owed him at least one more—he'd only come three times.

She'd also learned that it was difficult to envision him as a fraud—Brett Thornton was nothing like the arrogant, reclusive, secretive, unfriendly, party-deserting man she'd expected—and that she liked him. *Really* liked him.

Of course, that could just be the six orgasms talking.

There was nothing to dislike about *that.* Still, she'd be wise to remember that this giddy…infatuation or whatever it was, surely had something to do with the thin air and the cloud of post-coital bliss fogging up her receptors. It was fine to like him, but she couldn't lose sight of why she was here.

Which brought another wallop of guilt from the other direction. Damn it, she didn't like deceiving him, and although she hadn't told him any outright lies, neither was she being honest with him.

But hey, he hasn't been totally honest with you, either.

That's right. He hadn't mentioned his formula or the fact that every cosmetics company in the free world was wooing him. Or that he'd laid claim to an extraordinary product he'd yet to prove actually existed. No, he wasn't exactly spilling all his secrets.

That knowledge assuaged her conscience a bit, and with a sigh, she turned her attention to her text messages. As with the voice mails, they were all from her mother and sisters, except two. One was from Nelson, repeating his phone message, and the other from her good friend Suzanne Freeland, an interior decorator, who simply asked, "How's Dr. Thorn-in-your-side?"

She'd been surprised to realize that New York and Cusco were in the same time zone, which meant that it was after midnight at home. Given the late hour and the fact that she had no desire to get involved in any conversations about baby names or wedding disasters, she fired off a quick succession of text messages, the first telling Meg to relax and delegate—but not to her—after which she added a smiley face, the second informing Cindy that no kid would appreciate the name Butterfly, the third reassuring her mom that she didn't look like anyone's nana, the fourth to Nelson telling him she'd found Dr. Thornton and that she'd check in as soon as she knew anything, and the last one to Suzanne: He's not what I expected.

After sending the messages, she tucked her phone back in her bag, then stood and curled her fingers over the intricately curved iron railing. Closing her eyes, she drew a deep breath, absorbing the unfamiliar sounds and scents of this place so far away and so vastly different from her New York apartment.

Soft strains of guitar music floated upward, a slow, seductive rhythm that encouraged Kayla to sway her hips. Cool air brushed across her skin, and she breathed deeply, inhaling the delicious scent of some exotic food lingering in the clean mountain air. The view from her hotel room overlooked the plaza, but Brett's faced the other direction, his view a vista of the majestic mountains and dotted lights from the outlying *barrios* of Cusco and distant villages.

She heard the door to the room open, and after a quick peek over her shoulder to make certain it was Brett, she remained where she was, enjoying the music, knowing he'd join her.

Seconds later she was proven correct when he came up behind her, wrapped his arms around her waist, and nuzzled her neck with his lips. "Hi," he whispered against her ear. "Miss me?"

A hum of pleasure escaped her. Firmly shoving aside her shame and guilt and all thoughts of La Fleur and promotions and payback and formulas, she reached up and back to encircle his neck. "Hi, yourself. And yes, I did," she said, and realized with a start that it was true.

"I missed you, too."

"How did your food scavenger hunt go?"

"Very well. There's a restaurant two doors down. Lucky for us *sandwich* is apparently a universally understood word. I bought us each two, seeing as how we're working up such an appetite. I also scored us some bottled water and homemade brownies." His hands cruised up to cup her breasts. "But seeing you wearing my shirt…suddenly I'm craving something other than food."

Pleasure rolled through her as his nimble fingers unfastened the top three buttons then slipped inside the material to play over her nipples.

She leaned her head back against his shoulder and arched into his hands. "Amazing how great minds think alike."

"I liked that little dance you were doing when I came in."

"Oh? You mean this one?" She slowly gyrated her hips, brushing her bottom against him.

His low growl rumbled next to her ear. "That's the one."

"Hmmm. I can tell you like it…unless that's an ear of corn in your pocket."

He chuckled and skimmed one hand down, over her abdomen, then pressed her more firmly back against his erection. Kayla sighed and turned her head, her lips seeking his. He utterly disarmed her with a slow, gentle kiss, brushing his mouth over hers with featherlight strokes that teased and made her ache for more. Gentle nibbles turned into a lazy swirling of tongues.

He sank into the kiss with an exquisite lack of haste, deepening the intimate strokes of his tongue until her legs trembled and desire gushed through her, pooling low in her belly, leaving her body, which only moments ago had felt sated, tense with need.

While one hand continued to tease her breasts, the other hand coasted lower, inching up his shirt that she wore until his fingers curved over her bare mound.

He groaned. "No panties. And God, you're wet."

She opened her thighs and he thrust a finger inside her, dragging a long moan from her throat. Ensconced in darkness and the cool air, surrounded by the moon and stars and mountains, enclosed in the moonlit privacy of the small balcony, Kayla gave herself over to the seductive lure of his caressing fingers. The tempting persuasiveness of his lips trailing down her throat.

"If you keep doing that," she whispered, sweet, hot pulses of pleasure jolting through her, "I'm going to...ahhh..." He slipped another finger inside and pressed his palm right...ohhh...there. Her breathing turned jerky and she bucked against him.

"Going to what?" he asked.

But she couldn't answer. The combined stimulation of fingers tugging on her nipple and pumping inside her while his palm pressed upward to rub against her sex with an exquisite rotation, shoved her over the edge. Her mind and body spun away in a fast, hard climax that shot sparks of pleasure through her. Limp and still breathing hard, she mustered the strength to turn around. He wrapped his arms around her waist, supporting her weight.

Their gazes met and held. "Don't let go," she warned.

He held her tighter. "Not letting go."

"Good. Because if you do, I'll just melt into a steaming heap at your feet. Holding me up is the least you can do after turning my legs to the consistency of overcooked spaghetti."

One large hand cruised down to slip beneath her shirt and cup her bare buttock. "Have I mentioned how much I like overcooked spaghetti?"

She huffed out a laugh. "No one likes overcooked spaghetti."

He made a sound like a game-show buzzer. "Wrong. I do."

"You realize the orgasm score is now seven to three. My honor demands that it's your turn. You're going to need to keep your hands to yourself for awhile."

His fingers gently kneaded her bottom then coasted lower to glide over her sex, eliciting a gasp of pleasure from her. "I think you're asking the impossible," he murmured against her neck. "You're just so incredibly…touchable."

Good grief, he was doing it again, the erotic tease of his fingers over her swollen flesh sparking renewed interest in her every cell. She should be exhausted. Pulling away. Looking for "me" time. Instead all she could think about was how good he felt, how incredible he made her feel, and getting him naked again. And how much she wanted him inside her again. And again. She felt as if she could stay in this room with him forever—a crazy and totally unsettling thought.

Needing a moment away from his distracting touch, she shifted slightly and his hand cruised to her bottom—only a slight improvement as far as her concentration was concerned, but she'd take what she could get. Then she reached up to cradle his face with hands that weren't quite steady. The stubble that shaded his cheeks lightly scraped her palms. She stared into his eyes and slowly shook her head, a tornado of confusing emotions whipping through her.

"I don't understand what's happening to me," she whispered. "What you've done to me. I feel like I've been struck by lightning." The instant the words passed her lips, she wished she could recall them. Surely it wasn't wise to admit such a thing. Declarations like that did nothing but make men nervous.

But Brett didn't look in the least bit nervous. In fact he was slowly nodding while regarding her through very serious eyes. "Struck by lightning. Exactly. Since the first moment I saw you this afternoon. Whatever's happening to you is happening to me, as well. Which is good as far as I'm concerned—I'm not a fan of 'unrequited.'"

Relief swept through her. Neither was she. Unrequited feelings sucked. But then reality slapped her. Nothing beyond their time together in Peru could come of this. He was a smart guy—once he found out she worked for La Fleur, he'd put two and two together. A thought that distressed her far more than she wanted it to.

Forcing the thought aside, she asked, "Do you think it could be this place? Maybe there's some sort of magic in the thin air?"

He shook his head. Leaning down to nuzzle her neck, he drew several deep breaths. "No. Your scent...I'm certain you would have had this effect on me no matter where I met you."

A frown tugged down her brows. "What do you mean my scent? My cologne washed off in the shower."

"Not your cologne, but your *scent.* Of your skin. Your body. The unique smell that belongs to you alone.

Sort of like DNA for the olfactory glands. I strongly believe that human scent influences sexual attraction."

"So you like the way I smell?"

He leaned down and buried his nose against her neck. "Oh, yeah." Then he straightened and said, "We all have an aromatic effluence of our immune system—a biochemical bouquet of pheromones."

She frowned. "I thought pheromones were basically a bunch of phooey."

"Some people believe that and don't give scent half a chance. I think they're wrong." He hesitated, then said, "In fact, I know they're wrong."

"How?"

Again he hesitated. "My research. I've proved that pheromones aren't, as you put it, a bunch of phooey."

Her heart began to pound in slow, hard beats. Was this the secret to his formula? "How did you prove it?"

"After years of research in my laboratory." One corner of his mouth lifted. "But most recently when I met you. There's just something about the way you smell..." he leaned down, brushed his lips against her neck, then drew a deep breath. And groaned. "Delicious."

She turned her face and, burying her nose under his jaw, drew a deep breath. "You smell...luscious."

"You find my biochemical bouquet pleasing."

She nudged her pelvis against his. "Among other things." She returned his smile, then swatted aside her conscience and forced herself to do what she was supposed to do. Gliding her hands over his shoulders, she said, "So...tell me more about this pheromone research. I'm fascinated. Does it have to do with the breakthrough you mentioned this afternoon?"

He nodded. "It's proven to be a double-edged sword. I'll tell you more about it, if you'd like, but first how about something to eat?"

Relief swept through her at his suggestion, because in reality she didn't want…reality. She wanted this cocoon of sexual splendor, where nothing from the outside intruded on their intimacy. Wanted this inexplicable magic to continue for as long as possible. He'd offered to tell her, and that was good enough. She was content to wait. Because once she knew, she'd need to contact Nelson and report her findings, and in spite of the promise of perks, a bonus and a promotion, right now that was the last thing she wanted to do. The mere thought made her stomach cramp in a very unpleasant way.

"Something to eat," she murmured. "Excellent idea. And I know exactly what I'm in the mood for."

"What's that?"

For an answer, she rubbed herself suggestively against his erection. And watched his heat flare in his eyes. "Any complaints?" she murmured.

"Hell no, sweetheart. Not in this lifetime."

8

BRETT AWAKENED and opened one eye to look at the clock on the bedside table, not surprised to note it was 6:00 a.m. The same time he awoke every morning. Didn't matter what time he went to sleep, his internal body clock came awake at 6:00 a.m.

But unlike other mornings, today there was a gorgeous, naked woman in his bed, the back of whose lush, feminine form was spooned against his front. His morning erection nestled snugly against the curve of her spine, and her soft breast filled his palm, and her scent…warm skin misted with a hint of spent passion, filled his head.

Definitely a huge improvement over waking up alone. One he suspected he could get used to.

Closing his eyes, he breathed deeply, then suppressed a groan. She just smelled so damn good. And felt so damn good. And looked and tasted so damn good. Hell, she even *sounded* good…the teasing note that entered her voice when her eyes glittered with mischief, her smoky laugh, the way she moaned when he was deep inside her, that sexy groan she made just before she came. All so damn good.

He brushed his thumb slowly over her velvety nipple

and felt it pebble beneath his touch. Last night had been...incredible. Like nothing he'd ever before experienced. Sure, he'd had great sex before, had spent the night wrapped around a woman, but something about *this* woman made it all feel so much more intense. Passionate. In a way that simultaneously captivated and scared the crap out of him. If someone had asked him yesterday morning if he believed in love at first sight, he'd have laughed his ass off. The entire notion went completely against his pragmatic, scientific nature.

But now he wasn't so sure. Because *something* sure as hell had happened to him the instant he saw her.

That was lust, you ass, his inner voice informed him. Possibly. He couldn't deny that he'd taken one look at that transparent skirt of hers and all the blood that usually resided above his neck and operated his brain had gushed below his belt and settled in his groin.

But he'd felt lust before. Strong lust. This...this was more. His common sense, upon which he normally relied heavily, kept reminding him that now was a bad time to get involved in a relationship—he had important decisions to make regarding his career and future and he didn't need the waters muddied any more than they already were. And even if he were to get involved, he certainly shouldn't contemplate doing so with an Upper-East-Side princess.

But all that common sense didn't stand a chance against the way this woman had made him feel from the first moment he'd seen her. The instant he'd caught her scent. His reaction to her was, without a doubt, further validation of his formula. Proof that a person's unique scent, determined largely by their DNA and immune system, was a powerful aphrodisiac. Not that he'd required further proof, but the fact that he'd now personally experienced it was just the icing on the cake. How much more powerful would his attraction to her be if she used the cream he'd devised?

Would she be interested in his scientific explanations of the cream's properties? Or would her eyes glaze over with boredom as Lynda's used to when he discussed his personal research work? Did he even want to discuss his findings with Kayla—a woman he barely knew? He'd hinted that he would, but how much should he really tell her? He didn't know, but surely it couldn't hurt to reveal what he'd published in the scientific journals. That information was, after all, available to anyone who cared to read it.

He didn't doubt for a minute that his formula would work, but hell, he had to question how much more sexually attracted he could possibly be to her. A slow grin tugged at his lips. He didn't know, but he sure as hell wanted to find out. Another night like last night wasn't something any guy with a pulse would turn down.

Of course, tonight wouldn't be nearly as comfortable as last night. They'd had a bed—not that they'd exclusively used it during their sex marathon. Tonight they'd be on the trail, sleeping in individual tents. He knew two things damn well—one of their tents would go empty, and sleep would have very little to do with it.

Speaking of their hike…it was about time they got up. He had to pack his gear and check out of the hotel, and Kayla needed to go back to her hotel to do the same. Then maybe some breakfast together followed by the bus ride to the tour's starting point.

His gaze wandered over her glossy auburn hair and the ivory-smooth slope of her bare shoulder. So far he'd liked everything about Kayla, but it wasn't too difficult to like a woman who was witty, intelligent and charming in a restaurant, plus uninhibited in bed. Nor was it necessarily a challenge to exhibit those qualities while dining or having sex in the comfort of a hotel room. It would be interesting to see how an uptown girl did on the trail.

She'd admitted while they'd eaten their sandwiches that she wasn't much of an outdoorsy gal. That she'd never been camping or hiked anything more strenuous than Manhattan's streets. She attended yoga, Pilates and spinning classes, and clearly was physically fit. Still, he was curious to see how she'd react to less-than-stellar accommodations. If she proved a good sport and rolled with the punches, he wondered if he'd leave Peru with his heart still belonging to him. Of course if she turned out to be a whiny complainer…well, best that he found that out sooner rather than later. Before his heart became more involved than it already was.

But his gut told him she'd rise to the occasion. That he'd somehow discovered a buried treasure when he hadn't even been digging. His life was already getting back into balance, and the trek to Machu Picchu hadn't even begun. Certainly he was making up for lost time in the sex department. Speaking of which…

He ran his hand down her smooth torso, his fingers brushing over the curls at the apex of her thighs. Kayla made a soft moaning sound and shifted against him, her silky skin touching him from chest to knee. She then turned onto her back, her thighs falling open, an invitation he wasn't about to ignore.

His fingers glided lower, to lightly caress her soft folds. A long purr rumbled in her throat and she spread her legs wider, lifting her hips into his touch.

Looking down at her, he watched color slowly flush her cheeks, her breaths becoming longer and deeper as her sex grew wet. He slipped a finger inside her and slowly caressed her slick inner walls. She opened her sleep-heavy eyes and their gazes met.

"Good morning," he said, leaning down to brush his mouth over the soft plumpness of hers.

"It's definitely off to a good start," she murmured. Her hand moved down and stroked over his erection. "Hmmm. You seem happy to see me."

He groaned as her fingers wrapped around him and gently squeezed. "Very happy."

She turned her head and glanced at the clock, then looked back at him, her green eyes glowing with sensual heat. "You're an early, um—" she squeezed him again "—riser."

"We need to shower, dress, get our gear together—which will require a trip to your hotel—and I thought you might like some breakfast before we catch the eight o'clock bus to the tour's departure site."

She stretched sinuously and undulated against his hand, all while her fingers drove him crazy circling the head of his penis.

"Gathering gear and breakfast…is that the best you have to offer a girl in the morning? Especially when she's facing four days of severe roughing it?"

He lowered his head to lazily swirl his tongue around her taut nipple before drawing the bud into his mouth. "I might be able to do better."

She arched beneath him and gasped. "Oh, that's definitely better. What else ya got?"

"What else ya want?"

"You. Inside me. Right now."

"Are you always this demanding?" he asked, reaching for a condom on the beside table.

"Sometimes. When I really want something. But being naked with you definitely brings out the demanding in me. Is that a problem?"

"I'll try to make the best of it."

"Good." She snagged the condom from his fingers then in a lithe rolling motion—no doubt courtesy of her yoga classes—she straddled his thighs. He reclined beneath her, his avid gaze drinking in the gorgeous sight of her astride him, her hair in wild disarray, nipples erect and damp from his tongue, dark-red curls between her spread legs glistening with the wetness of her arousal.

"You realize I'm now going to want to be awakened in a similar fashion every morning we're on the trail," she said as she slowly rolled the condom down his length.

"So you're telling me you're not only demanding, you're spoiled, as well."

"Figured it was best to throw all my bad habits right on the table." She raised up on her knees, then slowly sank down the length of his erection. He sucked in a hard breath as her tight, wet heat engulfed him, sizzling lust along his nerves. When he was buried to the hilt, she looked down at him through half-closed eyes. "And if I'm spoiled, it's all your fault." She rocked her hips, her satiny inner walls clamping around him, dragging a groan from his throat as he thrust upward. "You've set an extraordinarily high benchmark. Be warned—you have your work cut out for you."

He was quickly losing his ability to make lighthearted conversation. "Yeah, making love with you is arduous work. I should be getting hazard pay." Reaching up, Brett filled his hands with her breasts, forcing himself to concentrate on holding off his climax until she came, a Herculean task given her control-sapping movements: rising onto her knees only to slowly sink down, a mind-blowing slide into sensual meltdown, then leaning back to clasp her ankles, gyrating as he thrust upward into her hot wetness, harder, faster, her grip milking him until the fight not to come was a battle he was about to lose. The instant he felt the first ripples of her orgasm squeeze him, his control snapped and with a ragged groan, he gripped her hips and pressed her down as he surged upward, thrusting deeper as his climax bore down on him like a speeding train.

His breathing and heart rate hadn't yet returned to the normal range when he felt her lips brush across his jaw. She lay sprawled on top of him, her face buried against his neck. His hands still gripped her hips and he remained buried inside her.

"Wow," she murmured against his ear.

"Wow," he agreed, unable to produce more than one syllable. Yet really, why try when that one described their latest bout of lovemaking so perfectly? Although, he couldn't quite ignore the unsettling realization that he'd completely lost control of himself and his body in a way he couldn't recall ever experiencing before.

"You were wrong, you know," she said.

"Okay," he again agreed, proud that he'd managed two syllables and too sated and lax to argue.

Her warm chuckle blew across his jaw. "You're very agreeable after sex."

"Yup."

"Good to know. Such knowledge might induce a woman to keep you in bed all the time."

"Okay."

Another huff of warm laughter. "Don't you want to know what you were wrong about?"

"Sure."

"You said '*good* morning.' That's wrong. It's oh-my-God, you-just-drove-me-out-of-my-mind-and-made-me-see-stars, freakin'-fantastic morning."

"I stand corrected."

He felt her lift her head and he forced his eyes open. Her beautiful green eyes glittered like jewels. "I feel—" she inhaled a deep breath then smiled "—incredible. Ready to take on the world."

"Good for you. I feel like I've been rode hard and wrung out."

"Honey, you were." She cocked a brow. "Is that a complaint?"

He huffed out a laugh at the way she kept asking him that question. "Hell, no. Except that you're now full of vim and vigor and I'm ready for a nice long nap."

She shook her head. "Typical man. Well, forget it. We have gear to pack. A bus to catch. Miles of rough terrain to hike."

"You're killing me."

She laughed, then pressed a quick kiss to his lips. "C'mon, lazybones. You'll feel better after a nice, hot shower."

His hands swept over her lush bare bottom. "I think

perhaps my strength might be returning. But if we take a shower together, we might never leave this room."

"We *have* to leave this room—and soon. We only have one condom left."

She squealed with surprise as he reared up to a sitting position. "Talk about incentive. Hang on, sweetheart." After she wrapped her arms around his neck and her legs around his waist, he snatched up the last condom, grasped her beneath her bottom, then headed toward the bathroom.

"Hmmm, it would appear the word *condom* has the same effect on you as *spinach* had on Popeye," she murmured, nibbling on his earlobe between words.

"So it would seem, although scientific logic would dictate that it isn't the word itself but the person saying it that caused this sudden boost in energy."

"Again, good to know."

"I don't suppose you know how to say *condom* in Spanish?" he asked, reaching behind the shower curtain to turn on the water.

"I don't suppose I do. But I bet if we went to a store and kissed passionately in front of the clerk, he'd get the idea."

"Problem is, once I start kissing you, I can't seem to stop. Instead of ending up with condoms, we'd probably end up with arrest records."

"True. Luckily I have an English-to-Spanish dictionary back at my hotel."

"So you're not only gorgeous and sexy and hot enough to set water on fire—you're also very handy to have around."

She traced his bottom lip with her tongue and his

body leapt to life. And he realized there was no point in even trying to deny that this woman posed a serious risk to his heart.

"Right back at ya," she said, her lips curving into a sexy smile. "And as soon as we get in that shower, I'll show you just how handy I really am."

He immediately stepped beneath the warm spray of water, knowing that his heart was quickly slipping from his grasp and not giving a damn. "Sweetheart, consider me more than willing to be shown."

9

FIFTEEN MINUTES into the three-and-a-half-hour bus trip—and she used the term *bus* lightly, as the vehicle was actually a van that looked as if it had belonged to a group of Haight-Ashbury hippies—to the hike start point and Kayla realized that she clearly was far too accustomed to luxury. Her butt was numb from the hard, worn, springless seat and she clung to the metal railing next to the open window—aka the air conditioner—with a white-knuckle grip. The wind whipped her hair across her eyes, a blessing because the less she saw of how close the vehicle frequently came to scraping the huge boulders that lined the bumpy road, the better.

The instant the driver had thrown the vehicle into gear, they'd zoomed off at what felt like a breakneck speed and her heart had lodged in her throat, a place she suspected it would stay.

Still, the scenery—when they emerged from the boulders—was breathtaking. A palette of greens and browns rising up the sides of the majestic Andes, set against a brilliant blue sky dotted with fluffy white clouds, the perfect backdrop for the array of small, picturesque villages they passed.

Besides the scenery, the only other good thing about

the bone-jarring, teeth-clanking drive was that it gave her something to think about besides the man sitting next to her. Or at least it should have. But somehow, even faced with the possibility of bruises and being shaken apart and splattered against a gargantuan rock on the bus ride from hell, her mind remained focused on Brett. On the incredible night they'd spent together. The extraordinary way he'd made her feel. And not just when they were making love—although there was no denying he was great in bed. And on the balcony. And in the shower. And against the wall…

She pressed her lips together and tried to corral her runaway thoughts. But he'd made her feel just as incredible when they'd simply sat and talked. He had a way of looking at her, of focusing on what she said, of really listening, that was extremely flattering. And very attractive. He asked insightful questions and offered spot-on observations, some serious, some humorous, and she found herself engrossed in just talking to him. Watching his beautiful lips form words. The man had the most distracting mouth….

She mentally looked skyward. Good grief, she sounded like a school girl nursing her first crush. Yet, how could she not, when that's exactly how she felt? Just sitting next to him on this bouncy, dusty ride made her heart race.

But now that they were no longer naked, therefore allowing her to think straight, she needed to get hold of herself and recall why she was here.

The formula. Dr. Thornton's miracle aphrodisiac wrinkle-reducing cream.

Problem was, it was nearly impossible to equate the Dr. Thornton she'd come to dislike in New York with

Brett, the charming American tourist whom she liked very much. Too much. So much that it seriously frightened her. Because in order to do her job, there was no getting around it—she'd have to be dishonest with Brett and also reveal anything he told her to Nelson. She could try to pretty that up and sugarcoat it as much as she wanted, but the bottom line was that she was lying. And betraying Brett.

And that was not sitting well at all this morning.

But what choice did she have? La Fleur was poised to join the ranks of the world's largest cosmetic companies, a step that would surely happen if they had a product such as the one Thornton laid claim to. Ensuring that La Fleur won the product would be an amazing coup for her—a professional feather in her cap that could open countless doors if her spying mission successfully secured Brett's formula.

And all she had to do was hide the truth regarding where she worked and why she was here. *That would be the lying part, Kayla,* her inner voice informed her. Oh yeah, and report any confidential information she managed to finagle out of Brett regarding the formula to Nelson. *And that would be the betrayal part, Kayla,* her inner voice coldly added.

As if she didn't know.

As if that didn't make her heart and stomach and, hell, her entire insides ache with an unpleasant sensation that felt like an allover cramp—the result of her conscience squeezing her.

Fine. So she'd compromise with her conscience. She wouldn't go out of her way to solicit information from him. But hey, if he *volunteered* the information, well, she certainly wasn't *deaf.* She could hardly slap her hand over his mouth and say, "Don't tell me anything because I'll use that information against you."

No. Especially since she was convinced that La Fleur really was the best company to manufacture his formula, provided it lived up to the hype. Which was one of the things she needed to discover. So, at least for now she'd assuage her conscience by not *actively* seeking tidbits from him, but if some happened to fall in her lap, well, all bets were off.

There. She felt better now. Sort of. Okay, not really, but it was the best she could do under the circumstances.

The bus careened around a corner, seemingly on two wheels, and she closed her eyes. When they were once again on a straightaway, she turned toward him and said, "I think they subject you to this bus ride before the hike so that the trek up the mountain seems like a piece of cake in comparison." She winced when her ass smacked down against the seat courtesy of a pothole of a size even Manhattan had never seen.

He chuckled and slid his arm more securely around her shoulder. The bus was filled to capacity with other hikers from various tour companies, two of whom they'd briefly chatted with prior to departing. The couple, Bill and Eileen Carlson, who Kayla judged to be in their late forties, hailed from Atlanta. They were going on the same tour as Kayla and Brett, but soon after the introductions, the bus had departed Cusco and hanging on for dear life had eclipsed conversing further with the couple.

"Definitely not the sort of limo an uptown girl like you is used to," Brett said, his eyes filled with teasing warmth.

"Limo, my ass," she replied, her teeth rattling. "I

don't ride around in limos. I walk everywhere. But you have to admit this road could stand a little repaving."

"You'll have to repeat that. I lost track of everything you said after you mentioned your ass, which is extremely fine, by the way."

"It's going to be sore and bruised after this."

"Have I mentioned I'm an excellent masseur?"

"No, but I'm not surprised. You have *very* talented hands."

"You inspire them. And a whole big bunch of fantasies, as well."

"I'd love to hear them, but I'm afraid we might bite off our tongues if we keep trying to talk."

"So I shouldn't mention that our tongues figure prominently in my fantasies?"

Heat that had nothing to do with the hot, dusty ride whooshed through her. "Why don't you hold that thought until we're alone, and then you can show me?"

He grinned and her nipples hardened. Just like that. Damn, what this man could do to her with a simple grin was nothing short of absurd. And…wonderful. In a way she'd never before experienced. In a way she was liking far more than was wise.

"I'll show you mine if you show me yours," he said, his eyes gleaming with mischief.

She laughed. "I've already shown you mine."

"I know. And I can't wait to see it again."

God help her, neither could she.

Thankfully the bus driver slowed down, lessening the stomach-lurching jouncing, and Kayla took the opportunity to pull her small cosmetics bag from an outer flap on her backpack.

"My lips feel like the Sahara," she said, pulling out her favorite La Fleur moisturizing lipstick. Before she could apply the soothing salve, he leaned down and brushed his mouth over hers.

"They feel good to me."

"That's because I wear this..." She held up the slim tube. "Although keeping it on my lips has been a challenge with you around. You keep kissing it off."

He stole another quick kiss then leaned back. "To use your question, is that a complaint?"

"To use your words, hell no."

She felt his gaze upon her while she applied the sheer wash of glossy pink color.

He glanced down at her cosmetics bag and a teasing light gleamed in his eyes. "Makeup? On a hike, princess?"

"Hey, a girl needs her moisturizer and SPF protection, especially in the sun-drenched mountains." After Kayla recapped the lipstick, Brett took the tube from her, his gaze bouncing from the flower image on the tube to the matching image on her cosmetics bag.

"La Fleur," he said.

Of course, he would know. But most guys wouldn't have a clue. So she swallowed her guilt and raised her brows, feigning surprise. "That's right. How did you know? Keeping your finger on the pulse of the cosmetics industry?"

A muscle jerked in his jaw. "I recognize the flower. Their ads are on billboards all over Manhattan. You like their stuff?"

A fissure of relief worked its way through her guilt. At least she could honestly answer his question. "I do. I'm sort of a cosmetics junkie—I love trying new products. Out of all the stuff out there, and believe me there's a lot, I like La Fleur the best."

"Why?"

"The purity of their ingredients. Their color palettes. I've found that some cosmetics companies will carry one, maybe two products that I like—an eye pencil or a mascara. But with La Fleur, I like all their products."

His gaze roamed over her face and he brushed the pad of his thumb over her cheek. "You have beautiful skin."

"Thank you. It's courtesy of La Fleur's coconut milk cleanser. It's amazing."

"If it keeps your skin looking like this, I'd have to agree." A frown bunched between his brows. "So you're really sold on this La Fleur."

"Absolutely," she said, meaning it. "Why do you ask? Looking to borrow my skin cleanser?"

Instead of smiling, as she'd hoped, he shook his head. "No. I guess I'm just...I don't know. Surprised maybe, although that's probably not the right word. I'm not crazy about La Fleur myself."

Trying her best to look innocent and feeling like a complete heel, she asked, "You've tried their line of men's products?"

"No. I'm just a soap-and-water kind of guy. I've had a bit of work-related contact with La Fleur and I was...less than impressed."

"They treated you badly?"

A sheepish look crossed his face. "Not exactly, although I did find them annoying. But I suppose not any more so than any other cosmetics company I've dealt with lately. But I just have a bad association with La Fleur."

Uh-oh. Nelson wouldn't be pleased to hear this. "Why's that?"

He hesitated, then said, "Because I attended a party La Fleur hosted and walked in on my girlfriend and one of their male models."

She blinked. Had he just said *girlfriend?* "What were they doing?"

He shot her a look that clearly said, "Do you really need to ask?" Then stated in a clipped voice, "She was giving him a blow job, and he was praising higher beings."

Dismay and sympathy flooded her, but then the significance of his other words dawned on her. *At a party La Fleur hosted.* The only party he'd attended that La Fleur had hosted had been...

The one she'd arranged.

The one he'd abruptly left, leaving her to explain his absence to some very unpleased corporate honchos.

"When did this happen?" she asked, needing to make sure.

"Two months ago."

Oh, boy. Well, at least now she knew why he'd jumped ship. And in a blink, all the anger and resentment she'd felt at his abrupt departure evaporated, leaving her feeling like a louse for all the bad things she'd thought about him. She'd considered that he might have had a good reason for leaving the party, and he certainly had. The fact that he'd left after making such a discovery, without causing a scene, amazed her. She doubted she would have been so composed in a similar situation, a realization that did nothing to make her feel like less of a louse.

Kayla reached up to clasp his hand that rested on her shoulder. "I'm so sorry. More than one boyfriend has cheated on me over the years, so I know how awful it feels, although I never discovered the betrayal in such a…graphic way."

"It sucked." He made a humorless sound. "No pun intended."

"You're not together anymore?"

His gaze turned cool and she immediately sensed his withdrawal. "No. I didn't care to be with a liar, and she, clearly, had found someone else. And for the record," he continued, his voice as cool as his gaze, "if I *were* involved with someone else, last night with you wouldn't have happened. I have faults, but cheating isn't one of them."

She squeezed his hand, instantly contrite. "I'm sorry. Really. I didn't mean to imply that you would." To her relief, the chill left his eyes at her apology, giving her the courage to continue, "What I really wanted to know, but asked very badly, was whether you're nursing a broken heart."

His golden-brown gaze rested on hers. "No. My heart is free."

His words zinged a thrill through her that her common sense immediately squashed. What difference did it make? It wasn't as if *she* would ever have his heart. Even if she managed to capture a small piece of it, he'd reclaim it pretty damn quick once he found out how she'd duped him. What had his exact words been? Oh, yeah. *I didn't care to be with a liar.* It would be very smart of her not to forget that.

But damn it, she normally wasn't a liar. Oh, sure, she wasn't above uttering little white lies to spare someone's feelings, but she'd never considered herself a dishonest person.

Until now.

Until Nelson, damn him, had put her in this untenable position which grew more unpalatable with each passing moment.

She pushed those thoughts aside, only to find them instantly replaced by a dozen questions regarding his former girlfriend. What did she look like, how long were they together, was she good in bed—the usual sort of info and details women wanted to know. She pressed her lips together and managed to suppress them. Whoever the woman was, she was an idiot, and out of the picture. Another thrill, followed by instant alarm, zoomed through her.

His grin flashed, but his eyes remained serious, searching hers. "At least my heart was free until *you* strolled along. I think I should call the police and have you arrested for stealing it."

Her pulse jumped, part with happiness and part with trepidation—because she felt the exact same way. But unlike him, she knew whatever they might share here in Peru had a built-in expiration date, courtesy of La Fleur and her role as corporate spy.

Forcing a light tone, she smiled and said, "I'm not too worried about being hauled off in handcuffs. In your attempt to report me to the Spanish cops, you'd instead end up ordering cold beer for the entire police force."

"Hey, I know how to say 'hot food' also."

"Great. You'd buy the entire police force an entire meal." She waggled her brows. "And I'd go free."

His gaze dropped to her lips and heat raced through her. "And I'd find you."

"You think so?"

"I know so."

"What would you do once you found me?"

He brushed his mouth over hers, a featherlight touch that teased and tantalized and drew a sigh of pleasure from her. "Before or after I got you naked?" he whispered against her lips.

Oh, my. The mere thought of him getting her naked tightened her womb. Before she could answer, however, the bus pulled to a stop. Dust swirled around them and the driver turned and smiled.

"Welcome to Quoriwayrachina," he said, the complicated name of the town where the tour began rolling off his tongue with a native's ease.

Brett looked at her and smiled. "Here we are, at the beginning of our Big Adventure."

She gazed at the mountains and lush vegetation and the groups of people standing nearby, readying what looked like tents. The beginning. Right. She just hoped she'd make it to the end of this adventure with all her body parts—including her heart—intact.

But one look at those intimidating mountains and then at the sexy man next to her and Kayla experienced some very serious doubts on both counts.

10

KAYLA STOOD next to Brett with the other nine people who comprised their group. Everyone went around and briefly introduced themselves. In addition to their guide, Paolo Trucero, there were Alberto and Miguel, Paolo's younger brothers, who were serving as the porters, and their sister, Ana, the cook for the excursion. All of the siblings possessed dark hair, deep-brown eyes, and friendly smiles.

Eileen and Bill Carlson turned out to be high-school social studies teachers who'd embarked on this trek—which they called the trip of a lifetime—as a gift to themselves for seeing their twin sons graduate from college.

"We deserved a reward and a vacation," Bill said with a laugh.

Another couple, Shawn Deavers and Ashley Laine, were newly minted college graduates from California taking a break before plunging into their new post-college lives. Dan Smith, a soft-spoken man traveling alone from Chicago, whom Kayla placed in his late fifties, rounded out the group.

"*Bienvenidos,* welcome," Paolo said, addressing the group after collecting everyone's tickets. "Today we begin our hike along the *Camino del Inca,* or Inca Trail.

This footpath through the Andes will lead us directly to the gates of Machu Picchu, one of the most beautiful and enigmatic ancient sites and important archeological finds in the world. I want to congratulate all of you on choosing this adventure, for this trail is the most authentic and scenic way to see Machu Picchu, to understand the Incas' extraordinary architectural achievement and their deep regard for nature." His white grin flashed. "And you'll have lifetime bragging rights against the *gringos* who take the train to the ruins."

Everyone laughed and he continued, "As you already know, the journey will be arduous, especially given the high altitude, but I guarantee that by the time it's over, you will not be the same. The mountain scenery, the exotic vegetation and animals, the Inca ruins, the dazzling cloud-forest vistas—they will all work their magic on you. We are fortunate that the high tourist season has not yet begun, so the trail will be less crowded, affording you the opportunity for the quiet contemplation this place inspires. I will provide commentary along the way, but please do not hesitate to ask either me, Alberto, Miguel or Ana any questions you may have. Their English is not fluent, but they know sufficient, like to yell, 'Hey, that *gringo* tourist just fell off the cliff!'"

Kayla's stomach dropped at his words, but again Paolo's smile flashed.

"Don't worry," he said. "That hardly ever happens. Especially when we obey the first rule, which is…?"

"Stay on the trail," everyone dutifully repeated.

"Excellent. I ask that you take a few minutes now to check that your gear is secure and that you have water and sunscreen handy. Then we'll be on our way, first crossing the Rio Urubamba, then beginning our ascent."

Knowing how her fair skin burned and freckled—the curse of redheads everywhere—Kayla slathered on another layer of sunscreen, then plopped on her floppy straw hat. She and Brett checked each other's backpacks to make sure they were secure, then faced each other.

"Here's to our Big Adventure and getting our lives back in balance," she said with a smile, lifting her palm for a high five. "No change, no gain."

He lightly slapped his hand against hers, then cupped her face between his hands. "Gotta tell ya, Kayla," he said softly, his gaze serious on hers, his thumbs brushing lightly over her cheeks, "I'm feeling changed already. As if my Big Adventure started yesterday afternoon at that outdoor café. And it's all your fault."

"Is that a complaint?"

"Hell, no."

A lump lodged in her throat. Because, in spite of her already sore butt and her trepidation about embarking on this way-outside-her-comfort-zone journey, she was happier than she'd been in a long time.

And it was all his fault.

Yet poking holes in that happiness was the knowledge that it would soon deflate, courtesy of her deception. Reality would hit once they returned to New York, so all she could do was live for the moment. And that's what she intended to do.

That and pray she survived this four-day hike.

Damn. Why couldn't Brett have decided to get his life back in balance on a tropical island adventure where the most strenuous thing anyone had to do was decide if they wanted a mai tai or a piña colada? A fancy hotel where "packing light" meant stylish sundresses and cute shoes and teeny bikinis folded in a Louis Vuitton carry-on bag. Definitely much more her style. As opposed to sleeping in a pitched tent and lugging a backpack. While she'd still be spying and deceiving the man, at least she'd be comfortable.

So much for glamour.

Sure, Brett had thought she was attractive yesterday, but no doubt his ardor would cool when after a few days on the trail, she looked like roadkill. She had no doubt that he'd still look supremely sexy—in that unfair way that men had of looking good while women seemed to…deteriorate. Well, her hat and oversized sunglasses would hide a multitude of sins. She hoped.

After everyone had on their gear, Paolo handed each of them a plastic-coated pocket-size pamphlet that unfolded like an accordion. "These show pictures of just some of the vegetation and the more than two hundred and fifty species of orchids that grow along the trail, as well as many of the birds and insects. You'll be able to spot hummingbirds, waterfowl and an extraordinary abundance of butterflies unique to this region. However, the most prized and rare sighting along the trail is the spectacled bear."

Kayla's insides chilled. *"Bear?"* she repeated, unable to keep the note of alarm from her voice.

"Bear?" Ashley echoed, earning Kayla's gratitude that it wasn't just her who didn't care for the word.

"Not to worry," Paolo said. "The spectacled bear is very shy—much more afraid of you than you are of it."

"I sincerely doubt that," Kayla said with feeling. "Did I, um, mention that I'm allergic to bears?"

Paolo chuckled. "This bear is an herbivore, so unless you suddenly sprout leaves, you are in no danger. The species is very rare and close to extinction. It is a sign of extreme good fortune if we see one."

"As long as we see it from a healthy distance," Kayla muttered, ignoring a sound from Brett that sounded suspiciously like a snicker.

They set out, with Paolo in the lead, followed by the Carlsons, Dan Smith then Shawn and Ashley. Brett and Kayla went next, with Alberto, Miguel and Ana bringing up the rear.

Brett entwined his fingers with hers, moving slowly so as to leave a gap behind Shawn and Ashley for a bit of privacy. "Don't worry. I'll protect you."

A frisson of annoyance rippled through her, stiffening her spine. *Humph.* Smug male. "I'll have you know I've been taking care of myself for a long time, thank you very much. So I'm used to more…uptown accommodations. Without bears. I'll adapt. And run fast."

"Sweetheart, you won't be able to outrun a bear."

She glanced over at him and smiled. "I don't need to. I only need to run faster than *you.*"

"I see. So you'd leave me behind for bear bait."

"No, I guess not. I'd protect you."

"Oh? I'm not the one who's, um, allergic to bears."

She narrowed her eyes. "Are you laughing at me?"

"Absolutely not." His lips twitched. "Are you allergic to hummingbirds, orchids and butterflies, too, princess?"

"Nooo, but I am allergic to annoying men."

Instead of looking abashed, his lips curved upward into a wicked smile, creasing that sexy dimple in his cheek.

The pad of his thumb drew slow, intoxicating circles around her palm. "You won't think I'm annoying when I'm massaging away all your aches and pains tonight."

She lifted her chin. "What makes you so sure I'll give you the chance to do so?"

He lifted their joined hands to his mouth and pressed his lips to her inner wrist. He gently sucked, his tongue swirling over the sensitive skin, and a soft gasp escaped her as tingles raced up her arm, melting all vestiges of annoyance, along with more than a few brain cells.

"That's how I know," he said softly, his gaze on hers, his breath cooling the damp spot on her wrist his warm mouth had left. "Because it's only been a few hours since we made love and I'm already impatient. By the time we make camp tonight, I'm going to be halfway to insane."

"Ah. The proverbial mad scientist."

"Exactly." His gaze ran down her length and unmistakable appreciation fired in his gaze. "Have I told you how incredibly sexy you look in your hiking gear?"

"Not since we departed Cusco almost four hours ago." She gave an injured sniff. "I'm feeling very neglected."

"You look incredibly sexy," he said immediately, placing another warm kiss against her wrist.

Dear God, she'd never be able to focus on the scenery if he kept that up. And speaking of looking sexy, she could sum him up in one word: *yummy.* Dressed in a pale-blue short-sleeved shirt, tan shorts and hiking boots that looked as if they'd trekked the globe, he looked rugged and tall and strong and muscular, and with his dark hair windblown and that hint of stubble on his jaw…

Yeah, *yummy* summed it up perfectly.

Kayla cleared her throat. "Thank you for the compliment, yet as much as I'm glad you think so, I feel compelled to point out that 'sexy' is not the way I'd describe myself while wearing dusty hiking boots, slouchy socks, khaki shorts and a plain white T-shirt, and lugging a bunch of crap on my back."

"Then you don't see what I'm seeing. Those boots make you look strong, like you could kick ass if you had to, and that's very sexy. And your khaki shorts show off your gorgeous legs and what I'm labeling as the best ass on the whole freakin' planet." His gaze drifted over her chest, and her already hard nipples tightened further. "And the way that plain white T-shirt hugs your breasts...have mercy." He leaned closer. "I'm going to have a hell of a time hiking with a hard-on."

"Well, I guess then you'll be the one ready for a massage tonight, won't you?"

"Sweetheart, I'm ready for one right now."

"Then you'll be very happy to know that I recently bought a book entitled *Mastering the Art of the Erotic Massage.* Fascinating reading."

The heat that flared in his eyes raised her temperature several degrees, as did the low groan that escaped him.

"Yes," Brett said, his voice a husky growl. "I'm very happy to know that. Your timing in telling me, however, is less than stellar. Climbing rocks is going to be damn difficult when I'm as hard as one. I might fall down and break something important."

"Don't worry. I'll kiss it to make it feel better."

Another low groan. "Okay, now you're just being cruel. How am I supposed to concentrate on the scenery when all I can think about is you? And kissing? And erotic massage?"

"Would it help to know that the book I read just prior to *Mastering the Art of the Erotic Massage* was *The Art of Sensual Kissing?*"

"That entirely depends on what you mean by 'help.' If you mean revving up my already raging libido, then yes. Unfortunately, it's not helping to relieve the ache you started with your talk about erotic massage."

"Can't be worse than the ache you started on the bus when you mentioned getting me naked."

More heat kindled in his gaze. "Ah. And I didn't even tell you what I plan to do with you once I have you naked."

She nearly stumbled. "Don't tell me. Seriously. I need to concentrate here."

"Good. Concentrate on the image of my tongue licking your—"

"Trail," she interjected in a desperate hiss, glancing around to make sure none of the other hikers could hear them. "I need to concentrate on the *trail*."

His sexy grin heated her down to the soles of her feet. "Right. On the trail I'm going to lick from your—"

"Truce," she said, with a shaky laugh. "I'm now officially hot and bothered."

"Welcome to the club."

"I vote we focus our attention on the *hiking* trail…for now."

"Good suggestion. Not sure how do-able it is, but I'm willing to try. Provided you behave and hold off mentioning your reading material until tonight."

"Deal."

Paolo halted, stopping the group. "We're about to

cross the river," he said. "The bridge is strong, but narrow, so we'll need to walk single-file."

They fell into a line, with Brett indicating with a gentlemanly wave of his hand that she should precede him. "Ladies first."

"How chivalrous."

"I'm a very polite guy. But honesty forces me to admit I have an ulterior motive."

"Which is...?"

His hand curved over her butt and she drew in a quick breath. "I really like the rear view."

Another wave of heat rolled through her at the intimate caress. Given the fact that the sun was beating down with ever-increasing intensity, she needed more heat like she needed a hole in her head. And what had happened to the truce they'd called not thirty seconds ago? Well, two could play at that game. As she moved past him to assume her place in line, she deliberately brushed against him and dragged her palm over his groin.

"Like the rear view?" she purred softly so only he could hear. "Good to know. I'll make certain you see plenty of it this afternoon." She gently squeezed him, enjoying his quick intake of breath. "Happy trails, handsome."

11

THE SUN'S waning rays were casting long shadows over the landscape when Paolo finally called a halt in a large clearing surrounded by dense trees and announced they'd arrived in Huayllabamba, the village where they'd set up camp. A collective sigh of relief arose from the group, one that Brett shared in. Shrugging off his backpack, he asked Kayla, "How do you feel?"

Her backpack and bedroll hit the ground, raising a puff of dry dirt around her ankles. "Well, let's see," she said, rolling her neck. "After hiking nearly seven miles in the high altitude—which is seven miles longer than I've ever hiked in my life—every muscle is screaming with fatigue and my back aches from lugging all that crap." She pointed at her backpack. "I'm hungry, thirsty, dusty, dirty and, in spite of reapplying bug spray every half hour, I still have half a dozen bug bites—I am sooo wearing pants tomorrow—*and* I can tell that my hair has frizzed into a knotty mess."

She paused for breath then shot him a smile so dazzling his breath hitched. "Yet, in spite of all that, I've never felt so...alive. So invigorated. My body is tired, but I'm completely exhilarated. With a deep sense of accomplishment. The thrill of having stepped outside my box to do something I've never done before—and living to tell the tale. Definitely a change, and I feel the gain."

Her green eyes seemed to glow. "Then there's the mixture of feelings this place infuses...the sense of history, of stepping back in time. It's part excitement, part wonder and part quiet serenity. And I also really like our hiking group. Very nice people."

She reached out and touched his hand. "One person in particular. I...I really enjoyed sharing this day with you, Brett. Experiencing the beauty of the trail, discovering the different species of plants, walking and talking with you. It was all...lovely."

Unable to stop himself from touching her, Brett drew her into his arms. She nestled against him and felt...perfect. In a way that made it very difficult to remember that he was supposed to be focusing on what to do about his formula and his future. That the timing was inopportune at best for all these unexpected and unsettling things she made him feel. That with her uptown princessy-ness, she represented the exact sort of woman he was desperate to avoid. But instead of listening to the reminders, he flicked them away as he would a pesky insect and urged her closer.

"Lovely," he repeated softly. "Yes, that describes it perfectly." Lowering his head, he lightly brushed his lips over hers. A jolt of raw heat raced through him at the brief contact, igniting him as if he'd been doused in gasoline then tossed on a bonfire.

He'd been fighting his runaway attraction to her for seven long miles, forcing himself to concentrate on the scenery, on the history that Paolo imparted, but Kayla had remained in the forefront of his mind. He couldn't recall the last time he'd been so painfully aware of another person. He'd found every excuse possible to touch her. Had known every time she'd spoken to someone else. Every time she drank from her water bottle. Used her camera. Tucked a stray piece of hair beneath her hat.

Her curiosity about everything she saw, the intelligent questions she asked Paolo, her humorous comments that made the group laugh, all attracted him like steel to a magnet. She hadn't hesitated to get down in the dirt and examine the tiny species of plants Paolo pointed out, nor had she complained once about the rigorous conditions. Instead she'd forged ahead, her face set with determination. She'd pushed aside her princess tendencies, swallowed her unease and fully embraced the adventure, showing courage and humor and a natural fascination with learning new things that both attracted and impressed him.

He also saw her kindness toward the other hikers, especially Dan Smith, noting how she made a point of chatting with the man during one of their short breaks. "He reminds me of my dad," she'd said in an undertone to Brett when she rejoined him after her conversation with Dan. "I sense he's very lonely."

"I detect something of a caregiver personality in you," he'd said, taking her hand as they resumed walking. "You would have made a heck of a nurse."

"Doubtful. The sight of blood makes me queasy."

They'd walked along, admiring the awe-inspiring scenery, sharing the stillness and serenity of their surroundings. The simple act of holding her hand had filled him with a sense of quiet contentment. The words *this feels good, this feels right* whispered through his mind. He loved the warmth of her smooth palm pressed against his, her slim fingers entwined around his. And, now, with the sensation of her in his arms, the place where he'd wanted her all day long, all the feelings he'd held at bay flooded him, and he bit back a groan of pure want.

"How are *you* feeling after a grueling day on the trail?" Kayla asked.

"You explained it perfectly. It was an incredible day, made even more so because I shared it with you." He lowered his voice to a conspiratorial whisper. "In case you can't tell, I kinda like you." He tossed out the words lightly, not sure if he really wanted to consider how huge an understatement they were.

Her eyes went soft and a gentle smile touched her lips. "I kinda like you, too."

Brett couldn't help but wonder what she'd say if he told her that there was no "kinda" about it—that he liked her so much it scared him. That she hadn't been out of his thoughts for so much as a single minute since he'd met her. That no woman, ever, had affected him so strongly, so quickly, both physically and emotionally. Not willing to risk it, he merely said, "Glad the feeling is mutual."

"It is. But I would have known you kinda liked me even if you hadn't told me." A devilish gleam glittered in her eyes, and she gently bumped her pelvis against his erection. "It's sort of hard to miss. With, um, *hard* being the operative word."

"That's not the only thing I like about you, but I obviously can't deny that on top of everything else, I'm feeling a little...horny."

She laughed and looped her arms around his neck. "That's only because you haven't seen my ratty hair under my hat."

He immediately plucked the straw hat from her head and dropped it on her backpack. Dark-red curls sprang free, sticking up in every direction.

"Were you struck by lightning on the trail?" he teased.

"Ha ha. You're hysterical."

He plunged his fingers through the soft, silky mess. "Very sexy…in an *I've-been-electrocuted* sort of way. Yesterday your hair was straight."

"That's because I worked very hard to make it that way. When I don't, it looks like I've been electrocuted."

Paolo cleared his throat to gain everyone's attention. "You all can take a few minutes to stretch and relax while we begin preparing the campsite. Since there are no restroom facilities here, I'll set up the bathroom tent first, which will take about ten minutes."

Kayla stepped out of his arms, and Brett had to press his lips together to keep from laughing out loud at her horrified expression.

"Did he say 'no restroom facilities'?"

"He did, but don't worry," Eileen Carlson said with a comforting smile from a dozen feet away where she and Bill sat next to their gear. "It's just like when you went to camp as a kid."

"But I never camped as a kid," Kayla said, with a hint of something that sounded like panic in her voice. "Closest frame of reference I have is when I went on one of those summer teen tours before my junior year of high school. We traveled by coach bus. We had bathrooms." She turned toward him, and there was no missing the dread in her eyes. "Did you go to camp?"

Brett nodded. "A different one every summer. Science camp. Space camp. Chemistry camp. My favorites were the ones where we got to blow stuff up. We had bathrooms, but we were guys so we used to go outside and pee in the woods anyway." He chucked her under the chin. "It's not that bad, princess."

"Uh-huh. Says someone who can pee standing up."

He shrugged and grinned. "One of the advantages of being a man."

She gave a derisive snort. "As if there aren't already enough."

"Oh? Like what?"

She crossed her arms over her chest and tapped the toe of her boot on the dirt, raising tiny poofs of dust. "You mean besides the fact that you don't have to deal with makeup, hair, high heels and cellulite? That gray hair and wrinkles make you look sexy and mature instead of matronly and wizened? That you don't have to worry about your boobs and butt drooping as you age? That the glass ceiling doesn't apply to you? You mean besides those things?"

He winced. "Okay. Filing my question under S.I.A."

"What's that?"

"Sorry I Asked. But, hey, men pay more for car insurance."

"Uh-huh. That's because men tend to drive like Mario Andretti—without benefit of an actual racetrack."

"You two sound just like Bill and I when we first fell in love," Eileen said with a laugh. "But be warned—we just celebrated our twenty-seventh anniversary, and we *still* have the men-versus-women discussion." She shook her head sadly. "Take my advice and save your breath, Kayla. Men just don't get it." She patted Bill's knee. "No offense, honey."

"None taken." He grinned at Brett. "I'm perfectly happy not understanding the intricacies of makeup and high heels. I prefer to just reap the benefits when Eileen uses them." He plucked her hand off his knee and planted a kiss against her palm. There was no missing the warm affection in his gaze as he looked at his wife.

It took Brett a few seconds to recover as Eileen's unsettling words were still echoing through his mind. Did she believe he and Kayla were in love? *In love*...the words gripped him by the throat and wouldn't let go. Is that how they appeared to other people? Would their fellow hikers be surprised to know that he and Kayla had only met...

Yesterday?

The reality hit him like an open-handed slap. How was it possible that she'd struck him so fiercely, so completely and quickly? That he felt so in tune with her, liked her so much, after such a short acquaintance? Was already thinking about continuing their relationship once they returned to New York?

He was normally much more cautious with women, especially lately, when he didn't know who he could trust, wasn't sure who wanted him for *him,* and who wanted him for his formula. But there was no worry of that with Kayla—she knew nothing about his breakthrough discovery. He'd experienced mutual attraction before, but nothing like this. So for him, there was only one logical explanation to explain the profound way she affected him, one fully supported by his research: their scent-communicating chemical compounds were fiercely attracted to each other.

Ashley joined them, her arrival interrupting his thoughts. She laid a comforting hand on Kayla's arm.

"Feeling your pain about the restroom situation, Kayla. I was kinda grossed out by the whole thing on my first camping trip, but Shawn's such an outdoors nut, it was either get with the program or find a new boyfriend." Her gaze flicked toward Shawn who stood a short distance away, engrossed in a conversation with Dan Smith, then she smiled. "Turns out I made the right choice. Just make sure you stay away from poison ivy and vegetation with thorns. And snakes."

Brett swore Kayla's skin paled. "Ah, yeah. You can bet I will. Yup. Absolutely." She cleared her throat. "I'm guessing that since the bathroom facilities are…primitive, a shower isn't available, either."

"Have buckets," Alberto called from where he was unrolling tents about fifteen feet away. "Fill from river. Dump over head." He flashed his brilliant white smile and pantomimed doing just that. "Good shower."

"Very cold," Miguel added, his smile just as wide as his brother's. "Very nice."

"Very cold, very *nice?*" Kayla repeated. "Clearly we have a translation problem here."

"Use bucket for shower," Alberto repeated with an encouraging nod. "I give you towel." He nodded toward Brett. "Man make you warm."

"Works for me," Brett said, struggling to keep a straight face.

"Me, too," chimed in Bill. "Hear that, Eileen?"

Ashley and Eileen chuckled, then headed toward the path where Paolo indicated the bathroom tent was now assembled.

"So you're up for one of these cold showers?" Kayla asked him.

Before answering, he stepped forward and drew her into his arms. "Sweetheart, I've been *up* all day long and could have used a cold shower long ago, what with staring at your gorgeous ass for hours. I took a few pictures of it, by the way."

"Of my *ass?*" She leaned back in the circle of his arms, her hands resting against his chest. "You were supposed to be taking pictures of the scenery."

"I did. I snapped a few pics of the flora and fauna, the ruins at Llaqtapata and your ass. What did you take pictures of?"

She laughed. "You're impossible."

"Better be nice to me, or man won't keep you warm after cold shower."

"Man better keep me warm or man won't get erotic massage."

He chuckled. "C'mon. Let's grab that bucket, a change of clothes and our towels. We'll get cleaned up before the sun goes down and it turns chilly."

While Kayla pulled clothes from her backpack, he walked over to Alberto who handed him two thick, white towels then said in an undertone, "After bathroom tent, big rock. Follow path this way." He curved his hand toward the right. "Private place."

Brett's brows shot up. "How private?"

"You be alone," Alberto said, nodding. "Always send hikers different paths to wash for privacy. No one bother you—unless you late for dinner. Then send search. Dinner in one hour. No be late."

He smiled at the young man, then said, "*Gracias,*" one of the few Spanish words he knew.

Alberto grinned back, then returned to his tent-pitching duties. Brett made a quick stop at his backpack, then, with the shower items in hand, headed with Kayla down the curving path leading toward the river.

And privacy.

12

IMPATIENCE PULLED at Brett, and he quickened his pace.

"Whoa, where's the fire?" Kayla asked, tugging on his hand. "Slow down. I need the restroom tent, but not bad enough to actually jog there."

Damn. The words *privacy* and *Kayla* had collided in his mind, and the almost painful anticipation of making love to her that he'd suffered through all day had instantly morphed into full-fledged rampaging desire. The knowledge that he wouldn't have to wait until they retired to their tent to make love had fired heat and lust and raw want to his every nerve-ending. It was all he could do not to fling her over his shoulder and break into a sprint.

"Sorry," he said, slowing down—an effort that cost him.

They rounded a curve in the path and saw Eileen and Ashley heading toward them. "It's just a bit further," Eileen said. "Good luck!"

"Okay, you know it's not going to be good when you need luck to use a bathroom," Kayla said with a sigh. Just around the next curve they came across what was clearly the bathroom tent, beneath a tall tree. The tent was nothing more than four six-foot high poles attached at the top and set in a square shape with white shower curtains hanging between them. A wooden plaque with the word Vacant painted in bold red letters was propped at the base of the tree.

Brett looked down at her, his impatience somewhat tempered by curiosity as to how she'd react. "Well, princess?"

She drew a deep, bracing breath, then squared her shoulders. "I'm not going to be beaten by a square of shower curtains. When in ancient Incan territory, do as the ancient Incans did. I'm going in."

"Atta girl. Except, the ancient Incans didn't have plastic shower curtains."

"Well, see that? I'm feeling lucky already." She cast a quick look around. "Keep an eye out for bears, okay?"

"Sure. Wildcats and snakes, too."

She narrowed her eyes at him. "Not helping."

"Sorry. I'll keep guard." His lips twitched. "While I remain standing up to take care of business over there." He nodded toward a nearby group of tall bushes.

"Again, not helping." After another scan of the surroundings clearly satisfied her that nothing harmful lurked, she handed him her bundle of clothes, raised her chin then marched toward the tent, looking like a solider heading into battle.

Chuckling softly, he moved a discreet distance away toward the tall bushes, his amusement increasing when she turned over the wooden sign so that it that read Occupied and rested it against the tree trunk. Five minutes later she emerged, then rinsed her hands from the bucket of water Paolo had provided.

"You okay?" he asked, joining her and rinsing his own hands.

"I survived. I'll certainly never take indoor plumbing for granted again. Nor will I ever complain about Porta Potties."

"See? It's all in your perspective. Sort of like the man who complained about his shoes hurting—until he met a man who *had* no shoes."

She looked up at him, brushing her hands dry against her shorts, and Brett stilled at her serious expression. A long look passed between them, then something flickered in her eyes. Confusion? He couldn't tell. Then, with a slight frown pulling down her brows, she reached up and rested her palms against his chest. "My perspective is changing," she said softly. "Rapidly."

Keeping his gaze on hers, he covered her hands with his, pressing her palms tighter against him, knowing she'd feel the quickening beat of his heart. "Changing in what way?"

She shook her head. "I don't think I can explain it. I just know I feel…different here. Weird as it sounds, I can feel myself, my ideas, changing." Her gaze searched his, looking for what, he didn't know. "Maybe it's all my gears shifting, getting back into balance."

"Which is good—getting back into balance is why you came here. Me, too."

Again, something flickered in her eyes, something that curiously almost looked like guilt, but was gone before he could tell.

"Maybe this place really is mystical," she said softly. "Magical."

Mystical? Magical? His scientific nature rejected the idea. Yet, he couldn't deny he felt different here as well.

As if she'd cast a spell on him. One that needed satisfying. Right now.

He drew her closer and kissed her, the way he'd been aching to the entire day. She rose on her toes, wrapped her arms around his neck and parted her lips. His tongue mated with hers, slowly exploring the delicious warm satin of her mouth. Fire licked under his skin, and his arms tightened around her, pressing her warm softness closer against his aching hardness. She opened her mouth wider beneath his, and he groaned, lost in a haze of lust.

The sound of distant laughter roused him and he slowly raised his head. Kayla looked as glazed as he felt.

"Are you as frustrated as I am by our lack of privacy?" she asked, rubbing her breasts against his chest.

He huffed out a humorless sound and curved his hands over her lush bottom, hauling her tighter against his aching erection. "Do you even need to ask? But the good news is that according to Alberto, privacy is just a short walk away. Everyone gets their own private bathing area and ours is down that path." He pointed to the right.

"Then what the heck are we standing here for?"

"Damned if I know." He snatched up the bucket which he'd stuffed with their towels and clothes, grabbed her hand, and headed quickly toward the path near the big rock. "You distracted me with that kiss."

"Is that a complaint?"

He smiled and quickened his pace. "Hell, no."

"Hmmm... Methinks you're just easily distracted."

"Actually, I'm not. Ask anyone I work with—they'll tell you I'm the least distractible person in the lab."

"So it's only when you're not wearing your goggles and lab coat that you can be led astray."

"I don't think it has anything to do with what I'm wearing, but who I'm with. *You* are very distracting."

"Another complaint?"

"Actually, I meant it as a compliment."

"In that case, you've scored a few more points for originality."

He grinned. "Always happy to score."

The path narrowed, twisting and turning for several minutes, the sound of the rushing river water growing louder with each step. After one last curve, it ended at a small indent in the river bank encircled by trees and dense shrubbery. A large rock, nearly waist-high, provided a natural fence of sorts, setting the tiny cove farther apart from its surroundings. On the opposite shore, a waterfall cascaded over a cliff, spraying silvery droplets which glistened in the waning sunlight.

"Beautiful," she murmured.

"Beautiful," he agreed. He dropped the bucket and towel and hauled her into his arms. "Alone at last," he muttered, then covered her mouth with his. She parted her lips, inviting him to explore, while her hands went straight to the button on his shorts—and the control he'd been forced to maintain all day snapped like a dry twig.

Lips clinging, tongues dancing, breaths panting, they tugged on each other's clothes, clumsy desperate fumblings interspersed with moans of pleasure and grunts of frustration. With tunnel-vision determination, he unfastened her shorts, then pushed them and her panties down her legs and helped her kick them off. He insinuated his knee between her thighs, spreading them, then curled his hand over her mound, his fingers sliding over her sex, groaning when he found her already drenched.

"God, you're so wet," he said, scraping his teeth along her arched neck.

"That can't be a surprise—this whole damn day has felt like foreplay."

He couldn't agree more. Every time they'd touched, every brush of their hands, each time they'd looked at each other, had notched up his anticipation.

"Hard and fast okay with you?" she asked in a tight voice, moving against his hand.

"Hell, yes. How hard and fast?"

"Give me all you've got. There's a condom in my shorts' pocket."

"I have one."

"Thank God. Putting it on now would be good." She yanked his shirt over his head and tossed it aside and he quickly unfastened his shorts and pushed them and his boxers over his hips. His erection sprang free and while he ripped open the condom, she peeled off her T-shirt and bra. The instant he was sheathed, he dropped to his knees, dragging her down with him. Desperation clawed at him, his own fueled higher by hers. He settled back on his haunches and she straddled him, taking him into her tight, wet heat in a single silky downward slide.

Raw need scraped along his nerves, and gripping her hips, he gave her what she wanted, what they both wanted. Hard, fast thrusts that beaded sweat on his brow and narrowed his entire focus to the place where their bodies joined. She arched her back and he leaned forward, drawing her nipple into his mouth. The scent of her arousal invaded his senses and he quickened his thrusts, bringing them both to the brink. With a ragged groan, she fell over, her body gripping him, grinding against him. The sensation sent him over the edge, and with a final thrust, he came, dropping his head in the warm curve where her shoulder and neck joined, as the jolts of pleasure shuddered through him.

He was still breathing hard when she said, "Thanks. I seriously needed that."

"That makes two of us." He lifted his head and looked at her. When their gazes met, his heart, still slapping against his ribs, seemed to skip a couple of frantic beats at her smile.

"You look flushed," he said. "And gorgeous. And sexy. And…wow."

"Dazzling me with those scientific terms again, huh?"

"Just calling it like I see it."

"Well, I feel flushed. And sexy. And wow. Thanks to you."

"You forgot gorgeous."

Her expression turned serious and she shook her head. "I'm not. But I have to say, the way you look at me…the way you touch me…you make me feel as if I am."

He leaned in for a kiss. "Because you are."

"Back at ya, Mr. Chemistry."

"You mentioned having a condom in your pocket—where did you get it?"

"I didn't just purchase film and water purification tablets when we went shopping this morning."

"You bought condoms?"

"I did."

"But I bought condoms."

"I know. I just wanted to have some of my own, so if I had the opportunity to drag you off into the woods to have my wicked way with you, I could."

"I like it. But you could have just taken one of my stash from my bag."

Something flickered in her eyes, and a dull flush crept into her cheeks. "I wouldn't want to go poking through your things. So I just bought my own." A half smile curved her gorgeous lips. "Besides, a girl can't have too many condoms—you never know when you might need one."

He'd bought a box of thirty-six—way more than enough for their hike, especially considering that privacy was at a premium. And if she had her own supply...an image of her needing a condom with a guy who wasn't him flashed through his mind.

An unpleasant sensation crawled through him, cramping his insides. As much as he hated to admit it, there was no mistaking it: jealousy. The thought of her making love with someone else, of her looking at another man the way she was looking at him right now, with teasing warmth glittering in her eyes, along with the lingering remnants of sated arousal...well, he didn't like it one bit. Not one damn bit.

Something of his displeasure must have shown in his expression because she frowned, then cupped his face between her hands. "You okay?"

Brett blinked away the unsettling image of her wrapped around someone other than him and forced a smile. "I'm fine." He ran his hands over her bare butt, and hauled her tighter against him, telling himself that the gesture wasn't as possessive as it felt. "Thanks to you."

"And thanks to me, we have another condom." She waggled her brows. "And I'm willing to share."

With him. Some of the unwanted tension eased from his shoulders. "Sharing is good."

"I agree. So why don't we share a cold bucket shower then see if we can't find a way to share the condom I brought?"

His fingers flexed against her soft skin. "Like I said, sharing is good."

13

"OH. MY. GOD."

The words exploded from between Kayla's lips with what little breath the icy water sluicing down her naked body had left in her lungs. Rivulets streamed down her wet hair, over her goosebumped flesh, and she clasped her arms around herself in a vain effort to stave off the chill. She glared at Brett, who stood—grinning, damn him—several feet away, holding the empty bucket. "That is *crazy* cold."

"It's a little chilly."

"A *little?* Feels like it came from a freakin' ice floe." She eyed his wet nakedness with a combination of flat-out admiration and deep suspicion. "You didn't say boo when I tossed a bucketful on you, nor did the frigid temperature rip the air from *your* lungs. What are you, made of steel?"

"Men possess more body heat than women." His gaze ran down her naked form with unmistakable appreciation. "Besides, looking at you supplied a lot of heat."

Teeth chattering, she grabbed her soap and quickly lathered up, watching Brett squat down along the river bank to refill the bucket from the rapidly moving water. A bit of her chill was forgotten when he stood and walked toward her, tall and leanly muscled, deliciously wet from the dousing she'd given him, and clearly not suffering from shrinkage.

When he stood in front of her, he set down the bucket. "Need some help?"

Before she could reply, he cupped her soapy breasts and flicked his thumbs over her hard nipples. Heat instantly shot through her. "You should have warned me how cold that water was," she said, trying to sound stern, an effort that was lost when her words ended on a low groan as his magic hands roamed her wet, soapy skin.

"If I had, you never would have let me dump a bucket of it over your head. And look at the fun we'd be missing out on now."

True. There was no way she could deny that his touch was incredible and warming her up fast. In gratitude, she slowly rubbed her bar of soap across his chest. His strong fingers massaged their way down her sore, tired back, dragging a groan from her.

He looked at her hands gliding across his chest. "You're getting me all in a lather," he murmured, leaning in to brush his mouth over hers. "In more ways than one."

Her gaze flicked down to his arousal which rose between them, hard, wet and so very tempting. She moved her slick hands slowly downward, palming the bar of soap, leaving a trail of suds down his taut abs. When she encircled his erection in her slippery fist and gently squeezed, he sucked in a hard breath and his eyes slammed shut.

Encouraged by his response, she grasped him lightly, moving her hand slowly up and down, from the base of his shaft to the tip, while she ran the bar of soap between his legs. A long groan escaped him, and he thrust into her hand, all while his fingers played over the base of her spine, which, no doubt about it, was highly sensitive.

"You know," she said, her voice husky with arousal, "this hiking gig is turning out much better than I ever thought it would."

"No argument here. Ahhh...that feels really good."

"This?" She tightened her fingers slightly around his shaft and circled the pad of her thumb over the engorged head.

"Yeah. That." His fingers slipped lower, over her buttocks, then between them to stroke her from behind. The soap slipped from her hand and she raised her leg, hooking it over his hip, opening herself to his wickedly arousing touch. Leaning down, he lightly grazed her neck with his teeth. "Really glad you brought that second condom," he murmured against her ear.

"Me, too. I only wish I had it in my hand right now."

"Personally, I really like what you have in your hand right now."

Her chuckle turned into a sigh of pleasure when he eased two fingers inside her.

"Still cold?" he murmured against her neck.

"No. God, no."

His magic fingers brought her to the edge, but just before she plunged over, he stopped, pulling his fingers from her body and a moan of protest from her throat.

"Hold that thought," he said, the glitter in his eyes letting her know he knew exactly where he'd left her. He moved to her shorts, snatched the condom from her pocket, then returned. After tucking their towels under one arm and lifting the bucket of water by the handle, he took her hand and led her to the large rock several feet from the riverbank where he spread the towels across the gray surface, then stepped up behind her.

Peeking over her shoulder, she saw him bend down, then a gentle trickle of cold water touched her shoulder, meandering downward, eliciting a gasp. He rinsed all the soap from her body with that same unhurried drizzle, walking slowly around her so as to rinse everywhere, the leisurely trails of cold water an erotically charged contrast to her overheated skin, invigorating and stimulating as they coasted downward.

When all the soap was washed away from her tingling skin, Kayla returned the favor, pouring a snail-paced stream of water over his body, watching the suds cruise down his taut muscles, leaving him clean, wet and more beautiful than any man had a right to be. His gaze never left hers, his eyes dark with desire, his chest rising and falling with his increasingly rapid breaths.

The sight of the suds trailing down his body, so tight with arousal and with his obvious effort to remain still, shot arrows of fire through her. By the time she finished, she was all but panting to feel him inside her. In spite of the cold water and the approaching chill in the air as the sun's light waned, she felt hot. Desperate. The folds between her legs swollen, heavy and pulsing. She dropped the bucket. It fell to the ground with a dull thud, and she reached for him.

"Brett…"

His name passed her lips, a husky murmur filled with the need she couldn't have hidden even if she'd tried, and the fire already burning in his eyes flared brighter. Without a word he stepped behind her, pressing his front against her back. Heat emanated from his wet skin, shooting fevered shivers through her. Helpless to remain still, her hips circled against his erection which nestled against the base of her spine. She heard his quick intake of breath, and he smoothed his hands down her arms, entwining their fingers. He then leaned forward, bending her body beneath his, setting her palms against the towels covering the rock.

"Don't move," he whispered against her ear.

"Who wants to move?" She felt him straighten, and in a haze of lust, heard the condom wrapper being torn open. Bent at the waist, she looked over her shoulder. Saw him roll on the protection. Their gazes met and held. Then, grasping her hips in his large, strong hands, he stepped behind her.

Anticipation that bordered on pain curled through her, and she widened her stance, arching her back, her body screaming for him, for release, as if she hadn't been touched in years.

His first thrust was a long, slow, delicious slide that dragged a ragged groan from her throat.

"Again," she whispered.

He withdrew, then sank into her again and again, his strokes leisurely, teasing, each one pushing her closer to a climax she desperately wanted, yet also wanted to postpone for as long as possible because he just felt…

"So…good," she said, her voice a throaty groan.

She surged back against him, and he leaned forward, blanketing her body with his. His hands came around her, one playing over her breasts, rolling her hard nipples between his fingers, while his other hand coasted downward, over her abdomen, then between her legs, teasing her sensitive flesh with relentless perfection while his body stroked deeply in hers.

The added stimulation of his fingers, his lips and teeth nipping along her nape, his deep moans brushing past her ears, shot her over the edge as if she'd been fired from a cannon. Throwing back her head and arching her back, she cried out, pulsing waves of pleasure roaring through her. She felt his body stiffen, and with a harsh sound, he thrust deep then shuddered against her.

She was still breathing heavily, aftershocks still rippling, when he withdrew and turned her around and gathered her against him.

His warm breath feathered across her cheek, and she closed her eyes, absorbing the feel of his skin against hers, the steady, rapid thump of his heart against her cheek. The gurgling rush of river water spilling over rocks and the distant waterfall provided background music, combined with the twitter of birds and the gentle rustling of the leaves. Kayla inhaled the scent of damp earth and cool water mingled with the musky fragrance of their passion clinging to his skin, and a sense of warm contentment suffused her. She felt sated. Relaxed. And happier than she'd felt in a very long time. Because of this place and the unexpected sense of peace it gave. And because of this man and the myriad of emotions he inspired.

Lifting her head, she opened her eyes. Their gazes met. Held. Neither said a word, yet she swore something passed between them. A silent communication that spoke of passion and intimacy and said more clearly than words that what they'd shared was...extraordinary.

Keeping one arm tightly wrapped around her waist, he raised his hand and brushed back the damp curls clinging to her cheek with fingers that weren't quite steady. "Kayla."

The way he whispered her name, with that note of wonder and reverence and desire, resonated through her, tightening her throat. She swallowed to find her voice, then replied with the only word she could. "Brett."

He lowered his head, and she parted her lips. Their kiss was a slow, deep, intimate, tender mating of lips and tongue, that now, in the aftermath of passion, soothed rather than inflamed.

When he finally lifted his head, he rested his forehead against hers, and said, "That was..."

She nodded, her nose bumping against his. "Yeah. I know." Then a grin tugged at her lips. "You know, sandwiched between you and this boulder, it occurs to me that I'm caught between a rock and a hard place. I'd always thought that was a *bad* thing, but in this case—" she heaved a happy sigh "—definitely a good thing."

He chuckled, then dropped a quick kiss to the tip of her nose. "As much as I hate to say it, we'd better get back. Alberto told me that if we didn't return in an hour, they'd send out a search party."

"Okay. But you may have to carry me. Once again you've robbed me of my knees."

He leaned back and his lips curved into that lopsided, dimple-producing smile that quickened her pulse. "Seems only fair. You robbed me of my wits. You have this very detrimental affect on my concentration."

"Really? Seems to me you're very capable of focusing on the matter at hand."

"I guess I need to qualify my statement—you have

this very detrimental affect on my ability to concentrate on anything other than *you.*"

Her heart skipped a beat at his admission. "Is that a complaint?"

"Hell, no."

"Well, in that case, I'm not sure whether to say I'm sorry, or Thank goodness it's not just me."

"I know which one I'd prefer."

"Well, I might as well admit it. If I don't, my nose will grow two feet, *à la* Pinocchio." She raised up onto her toes and gave him a fast, teasing kiss. "It's not just you—you have the same effect on me."

"Well, don't think for a minute I'd consider saying I'm sorry, 'cause I'm not. I'm damn glad." The amusement faded from his eyes, and his expression turned serious. "Damn glad I came to Peru. And that you did, too. Damn glad for the accident of fate that booked us on the same excursion."

The reality of her deception roared back with a vengeance, and the flood of guilt nearly drowned her. In the space of a heartbeat she went from post-coital euphoria to miserable self-reproach, all made worse by the fact that she really liked this man. More and more, with each minute she spent in his company. Which only served to increase her guilt more and more, and fill her with a sense of genuine distress because she couldn't help but wonder if their brief affair might not have turned into something deeper under other circumstances. As it was, she'd be an idiot to allow herself to become emotionally involved, because there was no doubt he'd walk away and not look back if he found out the truth. And if he chose La Fleur to manufacture his formula, he'd eventually find out.

But she had a very bad feeling that it was already too late, and that she was well on her way to being an idiot.

Shoving aside her guilt and offering him a smile that she hoped didn't appear as tight as it felt, Kelly said, "I'm damn glad we're on the same hike, too. And believe me, that's saying a lot considering the non-Hyatt-Hotel-like facilities."

"You're bearing up very well, I have to say."

"I can't deny I'm enjoying the challenge, and having to concentrate on something other than the family and work minutia that normally fills my time. And, of course, the promise of amazing sex at the end of the day is quite an incentive."

"Agreed. And now that we've enjoyed that amazing sex—"

"—twice."

"Twice," he concurred, "Let's take one last quick rinse, get dressed, then head back to the campsite to eat. I'm starving."

"For food?" she teased.

"Yeah…for now. After dinner, once we're settled in our tent, I'll show you what I'm really hungry for."

She smiled, but a cloud of doom hovered over her sunny sense of anticipation. Because with each moment spent in his company, with each experience they shared—both sexual and on their hiking adventure—the more she didn't want her time with Brett to end.

And the more she realized that she had no choice.

14

WITH ALL the hikers seated on sturdy logs set around a large campfire, Brett breathed in the mouthwatering scents wafting up from the plate cradled in his lap.

"For mountain dwellers such as the Incas," Paolo explained, "meat, served with potatoes, was a mainstay of their diet. But corn was their most important and revered crop. The food Ana has prepared for you exemplifies that of a typical Inca meal. The corn raised in Cusco and around the Sacred Valley was, and still is, called *choclo,* and was considered the finest in the entire empire, with large, puffy white kernels and a distinctive, sweet taste. Tonight you will enjoy it in the classic style—boiled on the cob and served with a wedge of mountain cheese."

"The main dish," he continued, "is called *lomo saltado,* which is strips of beef mixed with tomatoes, onions and potato chunks served over rice. She has also prepared *rocoto relleno*—a hot bell pepper stuffed with meat and vegetables. Ana makes the filling mild, but be warned, the pepper itself is quite spicy."

He smiled then raised his cup. "Tonight we shall drink one of Peru's most delicious beverages, *chicha morada.* It is nonalcoholic and the deep purple color is due to the blue corn from which it is made. But before we begin our meal, we shall observe the Peruvian custom of offering a sip of our drink to *Pachamama,* or Mother Earth, to show thanks for the earth's generous bounty." He tipped his cup and spilled just a bit, then raised it to his lips and drank.

Everyone followed his example, and the cool, sweet, drink slid down Brett's throat. He looked at Kayla, noticed that her eyes were closed as she savored the unusual but tasty flavor. Paolo then picked up his fork, smiled and said, "Enjoy!" and everyone applied themselves to the meal.

Under any circumstances, the food would have been delicious, but after such a strenuous day, capped off by mind-blowing sex—twice—Brett mentally dubbed the meal the Best Damn Food Ever. Everyone made appreciative noises and comments, to which Ana responded by smiling and thanking them.

Conversations broke out about the day's hike, with everyone adding their impressions and discussing what they'd enjoyed the most.

"The Inca Trail offers a cornucopia for the senses," Paolo said. "I invite each of you to tell what you liked best based on which of your senses was most engaged."

Eileen and Ashley chose sight, enthusing over the exquisite orchids, awe-inspiring vistas, and miles of deep-blue sky. Dan, Bill and Shawn chose touch, claiming they'd most admired the ruins at Llaqtapata, being able to run their hands over the centuries-old stones.

Brett considered for a moment, then said, "I'd have to choose smell. I've always been interested in scents, studying the ways they affect us. The combination of fragrances here—clean air, forest, sunshine and something else, something indescribable that is unique to this place—makes it smell…peaceful."

Everyone agreed that a serene atmosphere permeated the trail, and how, in spite of the rigors of hiking in the high altitude, they felt very relaxed.

"My favorite was the sounds," Kayla said. "The rushing river, the crunch of leaves beneath my feet, the birds singing, the branches rustling. Living in New York City, I never get to hear the sounds of nature."

While they continued to share favorite moments of the day, Ana offered second helpings and no one refused.

"This is incredible." Kayla leaned closer to Brett while forking up another bite of the savory beef. "How Ana managed to prepare such a feast in the middle of a forest, without benefit of electricity, boggles my mind. I couldn't hope to match something like this even with the aid of a professional kitchen and an assistant chef. I think she should have her own cooking show. I'll do the PR."

He popped a piece of the smooth, creamy, mountain cheese into his mouth. "You don't cook?"

She shot him a sideways glance. "Depends. Do you consider smearing cream cheese on a bagel cooking?"

"Depends. Is the bagel toasted?"

She laughed. "You're probably a good cook, what with knowing about combining chemicals and all."

"All that gives me is the knowledge to start fires in the kitchen—and, luckily, how to put them out. I've learned the hard way that combining chemicals in a lab and ingredients in a kitchen are two very different things."

"Here's something I don't tell everyone," she said inching closer and dropping her voice to a conspiratorial whisper. "I use my oven as storage space for my bread, cereal and cookies."

He shot her an exaggerated look of shock. "You mean it has other uses?"

"Not as far as I'm concerned. Who needs an oven when you have a microwave and dozens of take-out places within a two-block radius?"

"That's my philosophy," he agreed. "What kind of cookies do you keep in your oven?"

"All kinds, because *my* philosophy is—There's no such thing as a bad cookie. But my favorites are the hand-dipped double chocolate chunk biscotti from Delriccio's bakery on the corner near my apartment."

"Sounds pretty uptown to me, princess. I'm an Oreo man, myself. Although, I'm a sucker for anything dipped in chocolate."

"Me, too." Her eyes glittered with mischief and she sent a very pointed look toward his groin. "Which fills me with all sorts of ideas."

His body's reaction was swift and immediate and he had to press his lips together to withhold a groan. "I'm going to choke on my mountain cheese if you keep looking at me like that," he warned in a laughing undertone.

"Not to put too fine a point on it, but I wasn't looking at *you.* I was looking at your…" she silently mouthed the word *cock.* "And imagining it covered in chocolate."

Okay, who the hell tossed him onto the campfire? Heat sizzled straight to his groin. His fingers went lax and he dropped the piece of cheese he held. It landed on his plate with a soft thud, utterly forgotten.

"Are you *trying* to kill me?" he asked in a low, strangled voice.

Before she could answer, Ana stood and asked, "Who wants dessert?"

"I do," Kayla answered immediately, laughter dancing in her eyes. Everyone else chorused their yeses. The empty dinner plates were cleared away to the sound of many compliments, then Alberto and Miguel offered coffee and tea while Ana served them each a small, individual cake baked in its own ceramic bowl.

"It's still warm," Kayla said, wrapping her hands around the bowl.

"And it smells delicious," Dan said, leaning his face over the bowl and breathing deeply. "Chocolate. My favorite."

"Mine, too," Kayla and Brett said in unison. Their gazes met and they both smiled.

"After dinner the first night on the trail," Paolo said, "it is customary for everyone to share something of themselves, about their lives, with the group. Where you live, your occupation, your hobbies, things of that nature. And most importantly, what drew you to make this journey. It helps to bring you closer to the people with whom you are sharing this wondrous experience. Many times lasting friendships are formed on the Inca Trail."

He smiled, then continued, "I usually go first so there is no shyness. I was born and raised in Cusco and still live there, very close to the house I grew up in—the house where my younger siblings Alberto, Miguel and Ana still live. Although, they tend to spend very much time at my house."

"Pretty girls always at your house," Alberto said with a wide grin, and everyone laughed.

"And handsome men," Ana added, ignoring the scowls her brothers instantly shot her way.

"I teach history during the school year," Paolo continued, "and spend my summers guiding tours along the Inca Trail. I feel a deep connection with the history of this area, and although I've traveled extensively throughout South America, nowhere I've visited fills me with the same sense of tranquility as I find here. I look forward to every summer, to hiking to Machu Picchu, to renewing my spirit and filling my soul with peace."

He took a sip of his tea. "On a personal note, I am twenty-eight years old and not married, a fact my mother reminds me of every day." Everyone chuckled. "I keep hoping to meet the woman of my heart, but she has so far eluded me. Maybe someday she will hike the Inca Trail, and we will find each other, but since you all are couples or—" he smiled at Dan "—single gentlemen, this is not the hike." His gaze circled the group. "Who's next?"

"I'll jump in," said Bill. "Eileen and I hail from Atlanta where we're both high-school teachers. We have twin sons who just graduated from college, one of whom earned a degree in accounting and the other who plans to follow in our footsteps and teach." He glanced at his wife, and took her hand. "We love the outdoors and discovering new places and have looked forward to this trip for a long time."

"We'd actually planned to visit Machu Picchu two summers ago," Eileen added, "but had to postpone our plans when I was diagnosed with breast cancer. It was a scary time and definitely gave both of us an appreciation for what's really important." She laid her hand over Bill's and smiled at the group. "I'm happy to report that I'm now cancer-free and very happy to be here—literally and figuratively."

The entire group gave her a whooping round of applause, and with a laugh, she stood and bowed.

Since Shawn sat next to Eileen, he volunteered to go next. "I grew up in Pennsylvania, the oldest of six kids—all girls except me—in a house that had *one* bathroom." A murmur of male-voiced sympathy rose from the group, and Shawn nodded. "Dudes, it was *harsh.* Me and my dad, we didn't stand a chance. With all those kids, my folks couldn't afford fancy vacations, so we went camping. It was cheap, and I loved it because I could escape my sisters in the woods." He wrapped his arm around Ashley. "This is the first girl I ever went camping with who I wasn't related to and who I didn't want to get away from. I graduated from college last month, and this trip is my graduation present to myself, and the first time I've ever gone anywhere that required a passport. Next week I'm starting a new job—my new career—and it's kinda scary, this whole being a responsible adult instead of a college student. But this week is for me." He hugged Ashley closer. "Me and my best girl."

"Okay, everyone say 'awww,'" Paolo said in a teasing voice, and everyone chimed in.

"I graduated with Shawn," Ashley said, "but unlike him, I wasn't much of a camper until he came along. I grew up in Idaho, near Sun Valley, so I'm a skier. Not being a college student any longer is…weird. On the one hand, I feel very grown-up and look forward to starting my career, but on the other hand, I'm scared to death because now I'm in the real world." She made air quotes around the last two words. "It's sort of like walking on a high wire without a safety net beneath you. I came on this trip with Shawn because I love going places with him. We've been together three years, and he's taught me how great sleeping under the stars, communing with nature can be. I'd rather be in a tent with him than in a fancy hotel with someone else."

Everyone clapped and again said, "awww," to which Ashley smiled and buried her face in Shawn's collar.

"I guess I'm next," Brett said. He wasn't sure if it was sharing this campfire under the stars, or the day of hiking, or the meal, or all three, but he felt an undeniable bond of camaraderie with this group of strangers. And a sudden, strong need to unburden himself.

"I'm from New York, and I came here to escape the chaos my life's been over the past four months," he said slowly, but then the words came faster. "I'm a scientist, a chemist. After I published my findings on a new skincare formula I developed, everything just went... crazy."

He rested his forearms on his knees, clasped his hands together and stared into the fire, reliving the insanity that had been thrust upon him. "Everyone wanted a piece of the formula. At first, I can't deny that the attention was flattering—it was the sort of recognition most scientists dream of yet never receive.

"But it quickly spun out of control. I was being pulled in too many directions by too many people. I didn't know who I could trust or what was best for my future and career. The pursuit by various cosmetic firms was relentless, and I couldn't stand it any more. I'd read an article about getting your life back in balance, and one of the things it recommended was going somewhere you've never been, to do something you've never done. I'd always been interested in Machu Picchu, so I packed my bag and here I am. And I have to say, this is the most peaceful I've felt in months." His gaze flicked to Kayla. "And the happiest I've been in a very long time."

He drew a deep breath, and a profound sense of relief filled him, as if he'd carried a stack of anvils on his shoulders and they'd now evaporated. Into the clear, brisk, mountain air. He looked at Kayla and smiled. "Your turn."

She moistened her lips, and Brett noted that she seemed rather uncomfortable. "I'm also from New York, and I actually read that same article as Brett, about re-balancing your life by doing something totally new, and believe me, a four-day hike in the Andes is about as far outside my comfort zone as you can get. So, here I am, an escapee from the daily stress of my public-relations job and high-maintenance family. And in spite of being so far outside my usual box, I'm feeling very…peaceful."

"I would suggest it is *because* you are so far outside your usual box that you're feeling this peace," Paolo said. "It is a common phenomenon on the journey to Machu Picchu. These trails, where the Inca once walked and lived, possess the power to infuse each of you with serenity, to help you find what you seek if you allow it." He turned to Dan. "You have the honor of going last, *señor.*"

Dan hesitated several seconds, then combed his fingers through his short, military-cut gray hair. "Well, I wasn't going to tell anyone, but since you all have been so honest, I don't feel right not extending that same honesty back."

Kayla shifted on the log beside him, and, noting her

frown, Brett scooted closer, wrapping his arm around her shoulder.

"I lost my wife three years ago," Dan said, staring into the fire's dancing red and gold flames. "Car crash. Hit by a drunk driver. He's in jail now, but that doesn't bring Marcie back. We were married thirty-five years."

Brett felt Kayla stiffen beneath his arm, then, along with everyone else, murmur her sympathy for Dan's loss. He could almost feel the waves of sadness rolling off the man and compassion filled him. His parents had recently celebrated their thirty-eighth anniversary. They were like two halves of a whole, and he couldn't imagine either one of them losing the other.

"We have two daughters," Dan continued, in a strained voice. "Both are married, and lucky for me they don't live too far away. I get to see them and my grandchildren often, which has made things a little easier."

He fell silent for several seconds, and it was obvious he was gathering his composure. After clearing his throat, he said, "Six months ago, my eyes started bothering me. Can't deny I hadn't kept up with regular doctor appointments after Marcie was gone. Oh, I did my normal exercises—racquetball and golf—but I didn't bother with annual check-ups until my eyes began to trouble me. Doc told me I have macular degeneration. In simplest terms, it's an incurable eye disease that leads to blindness. He gives me a year, two at most, before my eyesight will essentially be gone."

Dan studied his clasped hands, and the only sound was the snap and pop of the flames. "Me and Marcie, we loved to travel. That woman was never so happy as when she was packin' a suitcase. Went somewhere new every summer. When the girls were growing up, we took them with us, and after they left home, we went on our own. Had a long list of all the places we wanted to see together. She kept it hung right on the refrigerator, and every year we'd cross off a new place."

He lifted his head and once again stared into the flames. "I'm trying to see as many of those places as I can in this next year. While I still can see them. So I can tell Marcie what they looked like. Hiking to Machu Picchu was on our list. So…here I am."

No one spoke for several long seconds, then Kayla rose. Brett looked up at her and stilled when he saw that her eyes were bright with tears, her cheeks glistening with silvery wet tracks. She sat down next to Dan, taking the older man's hand in hers.

"I'm so sorry, Dan," she said, in a low voice. "My father…he died in nearly the same way. Car crash. Hit by a teenager high on drugs. I know how much it hurts. How hard it is to talk about."

Tears misted Dan's eyes and his head jerked in a tight nod. "Rips my heart out every time."

"I know." Fresh tears rolled down her cheek, and Brett's heart squeezed tight. For her. And for Dan. He couldn't imagine the pain of losing a loved one under such tragic circumstances. "What you're doing," she said softly, her gaze steady on Dan's, "traveling to the places you and Marcie wanted to go…I hope you'll get to see all of them. For both your sakes."

"Me, too, Dan," said Eileen, and Brett and the others chimed in with similar sentiments.

Dan pressed his lips together then cleared his throat. "Thank you. All of you. I appreciate the kind words."

He gave a shaky smile. "But I feel like I've cast a pall over the party."

"No," Paolo said quickly. "It is in the talking about our lives, in the sharing of our hopes and dreams and pains that we find answers and comfort and peace. And those can often be found not only in those closest to us, but in the presence of strangers, as well."

Paolo rose and swept his hand toward the area behind them. "Your tents are all prepared, and you will find a flashlight in each one. You can retire, or remain around the fire if you wish. There is water in the kitchen tent for teeth-brushing and face-washing. Please do not wander from the campsite, nor go any further away than the bathroom tent. Normally we break up into two groups at this time—men and women. Ana will escort the ladies to the bathroom while the men brush their teeth here, then we'll switch. After that, if you go anywhere, bring your flashlight and do not go alone. If you need anything or experience any problems, do not hesitate to awaken me or Alberto, Ana or Miguel. We will wake you early to begin our second day, which, I will warn you, is the most difficult day of the hike. I wish you all a good night and a good sleep."

Everyone rose and made their way toward the tents. Brett's gaze remained fixed on Kayla and his insides tightened with sympathy at her bleak expression. Clearly talking about the circumstances of her father's death had upset her. She reminded him of a deflated balloon. He approached her slowly, uncertain of what to say or do and cursed his inexperience in dealing with such a situation. Certainly the least he could do was offer his sympathy.

Before he could speak, however, she raised her damp gaze to his and said in a voice that sounded so sad and inexorably weary, it broke his heart, "After the bathroom break...I'm sorry, but I think I'd like to just go to sleep." Without another word, she headed toward her tent, which he noted was next to the one outside which his gear was stacked.

She looked so...lost, so tired and upset. Sympathy and an entire flood of other feelings he couldn't name washed through him as he watched her dejected form disappear down the path toward the bathroom tent, following Ana and the other women. He wanted to comfort her, to erase that bleak sadness from her beautiful eyes, but he didn't know how, especially without it seeming as if his ulterior motive was to get her into bed.

And while Brett couldn't name the unsettling feelings coursing through him, the very depth at which they grabbed him and wouldn't let go scared the living daylights out of him.

15

WITH THE washing-up and teeth-brushing finished, Kayla should have been ready to crawl into her tent and pass out cold from weariness. Yet as achingly tired as her body was, her mind was revving at full speed and she knew sleep wouldn't come. The memories had escaped from the corner of her soul where she normally kept them carefully locked away, and she knew from experience that there'd be no putting them back to rest until she'd dealt with them.

Adding to her distress was her promise to Brett of a massage and spending the night together, but she simply felt too drained to deliver, both emotionally and physically. Which would leave him in the lurch and quite possibly piss him off. But it was just as well. It wasn't as if their affair could go anywhere. What difference did it make if it ended now or three days from now?

It shouldn't make a difference, damn it, but the fact that it did indicated that she'd foolishly allowed herself to become emotionally involved. Which, if it were with anyone other than Brett, wouldn't be a problem. But with Brett—a man she'd lied to since the moment she'd met him? *Big* problem.

Kneeling in front of her tent, she glanced around,

noting that everyone was settling in for the night. Her gaze settled on Ashley, who was squeezing her sleeping bag into Shawn's small tent. She looked up, saw Kayla and waved goodnight. Kayla returned the gesture, then turned toward Brett's tent. The flaps were closed. Probably he'd already turned in.

Was he upset with her? Most likely, and she didn't blame him. She glanced around and barely made out Ana in the shadows of the kitchen tent. After putting away her toiletries, she unrolled her sleeping bag, but the thought of lying down didn't appeal at all. She glanced over her shoulder at the still-crackling fire and rose to her feet.

Stepping over the log that served as a bench, she sank to the ground and rested her back against the thick, rounded wood. She drew up her legs, wrapped her arms around her knees, and stared into the dancing flames, trying to empty her mind, but failing completely.

Several minutes passed, the murmurs of voices quieting down until the only sound that remained was that of the fire. Warmth from the flames eased over her body, but did nothing to warm the sad, lonely chill in her heart.

Footsteps sounded behind her. She turned and stilled at the sight of Brett, holding a plastic mug from which a tempting curl of steam rose. He stared down at her for several seconds, then moved forward, stepping over the log to stand in front of her. Hunkering down on his haunches, he extended the cup.

"It's tea," he said, his voice filled with quiet concern that matched the look in his eyes. "I thought maybe you'd like something hot and soothing to drink."

"Thank you." She barely managed to push the words

past the lump that lodged in her throat at the kind gesture. Wrapping her cold hands around the warm mug, she forced herself to meet his gaze. "Brett, I'm sorry—"

He touched his fingers to her lips, stopping her words. "Please don't apologize. There's no need. I'm the one who's sorry. For not knowing what to say or do to comfort you." His fingers slid away and he regarded her through very serious eyes. "If you'd like some company, someone to talk to, or even just to sit silently with you so you're not out here alone, I'd be happy to join you. But if you want to be alone, I understand."

To her mortification, hot tears welled in her eyes. She looked away, but he'd clearly seen the sheen because he reached into the back pocket of his jeans and pulled out a hanky.

"Here you go," he said, handing her the folded white square.

As she had no tissues, Kayla set down her mug, accepted the offering and wiped her face. "I didn't know men still carried hankies."

"Habit I picked up from my grandfather. Came in handy while growing up because I always seemed to have a head cold." One corner of his mouth quirked upward. "You can imagine what a babe magnet I was."

A huff of unexpected laughter escaped her. "You clearly improved with age."

"Thanks. But believe me, I had nowhere to go but up."

She made another swipe under her eyes which, much to her embarrassment, continued to leak silent tears. "You know, in spite of overwhelming evidence to the contrary, I'm not a weepy female."

"I believe you."

Based on the sincerity in his gaze, he did. Which only made her feel worse because while her "I'm not a weepy female" statement was true—usually—she'd deceived him from the moment they'd met. She certainly didn't deserve to have him believe her. This brought on a fresh onslaught of tears. Damn it, she hoped she'd run out soon.

He reached out and took the hanky from her less-than-steady fingers, then gently dabbed at her eyes. "Jesus, Kayla, you're breaking my heart. Tell me what I can do to help. To make you feel better. I don't want to leave you like this. Can I sit with you?"

"Don't most men normally run away from crying women?"

"I guess I'm not most men."

No, it appeared he wasn't, which should have thrilled her, but only served to heap another layer of guilt on her already mile-high stack.

She should have told him to go to bed. Released him from any misguided sentiments of chivalry he harbored about leaving her alone. But the thought of being alone with her thoughts filled her with a crushing ache that made it feel as if a mountain sat on her chest.

"I wouldn't mind the company," she said, "but I know you must be tired, so if you'd rather go to sleep…"

Her words petered off when, without any hesitation, he moved next to her, propping his back against the log. He stretched out his long legs, crossed his ankles, and tucked his hands in his jacket pockets. She realized that the fact he'd been so careful not to brush against her, to touch her in any manner, was his silent way of letting her know he wasn't looking for sex. She quickly picked up the mug of tea to hide more tears at his thoughtfulness.

They sat together, the quiet broken only by the fire's lively snaps and the rustling of leaves in the cool wind. It was a companionable silence, one that comforted her rather than making her feel as if she had to say something, anything, to fill an awkward lull in the conversation. A silence that allowed her to regain control of her emotions and put to rest the profound sense of sadness that had swamped her.

She knew from the grief counseling she'd sought after her father's death that the best way for her to grieve was not to try and stop the emotions, but to allow them to wash over her, then let them go. Then she could carefully pack them away again.

She tilted her head back, stared at the glittering stars, and sipped her tea. By the time the mug was empty, Kayla felt fully composed, and after drawing a deep breath, said softly, "When I was a kid, we'd have a cookout every Sunday during the summer. It was always an event. The neighbors who lived on either side of us came every week, the dads carting over beer and burgers, the moms bringing huge bowls of homemade potato and macaroni salads. We always had it at our house because we had an above-ground pool. While all the kids splashed around, the moms chatted over chips and dip, while the dads hovered around the grill, with my dad as the head chef. He knew how to grill a mean burger."

A smile tugged at her lips. "After dinner—which always tasted better after a few hours in the pool—the dads would jump in the water with us and make waves. The bigger the better.

"Then, when dusk settled, we'd catch fireflies. Dessert was marshmallows roasted over the charcoal grill. After stuffing ourselves with gooey sweetness, we'd sit on the lawn and look up at the stars, picking out the constellations. I remember when I was about five asking my dad what stars were. He told me they were tiny magical lights that lit the night sky, that everyone could see, no matter where in the world they were. So that even if we weren't in the same place, like when he had to travel on business, I could look up and see the same stars he was looking at. And that way we'd always be together."

She stared at twinkling diamond-like lights. "I wonder if he's looking at the stars now."

She hadn't even realized she'd said those last words out loud until Brett said, softly, "I bet he is. And knows that you are, too."

Her heart swelled at his comment. "Did you look at the stars when you were a kid?"

"Oh, yeah. Still do. Of course, when I was five and asked my dad what stars are, he said, 'They're self-gravitating massive spheres of plasma in hydrostatic equilibrium which generate their own energy through the process of nuclear fusion.'"

For the first time since he'd sat next to her, she turned to stare at him and saw he was gazing up at the night sky. "You're kidding."

He looked her way, and his mouth slanted upward in that dimple-producing lopsided grin. "I'm not. But considering that he's an astrophysicist, his answer wasn't surprising. Now if I'd asked my mother, who's an artist, I'm sure I would have gotten a more whimsical answer."

"An astrophysicist and an artist. That's quite an interesting combination."

"They're quite an interesting couple. They met at college when my dad, who tends to forget where he's going when he's mulling over a scientific problem, wandered into the wrong classroom. Instead of organic chemistry, he found himself in Nude Painting 101."

A giggle tickled her throat. "That must make for an interesting how-I-met-your-mother story."

"Sure does." He grinned. "Especially since Mom was the model."

Kayla felt her eyes widen, then she laughed. "Clearly she made quite a first impression."

"Yup. She was the proverbial starving artist and used to model for the class to pay her tuition. Dad says he took one look at her and it was if an explosion of supernova proportions occurred. Which is saying a lot since a stellar explosion is estimated to release an equivalent energy of up to one million trillion trillion megatons of TNT."

"Wow. That's some big kaboom."

"That's what Dad said—once he remembered how to speak English."

"Sounds like you have a nice relationship with your folks."

"I do. They're good people."

Pulling her gaze from his, she once again stared into the fire. "I miss my dad every day," she said softly, an image of her dad's smiling face flashing through her mind, "but I've learned to live with the loss, with the way he died. I rarely let it get the better of me anymore like I did tonight. But sometimes it hits me. Blindsides me. Like when Dan mentioned his wife. I didn't expect it and it all came roaring back. The mind-numbing grief.

The senselessness of it all. The fury at the person who took my dad away. And the aftermath…"

She squeezed her eyes shut, and tried to stop the flow of words, but now that the floodgates were open, she couldn't. "The trial…it was a nightmare. The kid who killed him was only eighteen. He's twenty-three now and was released from jail more than two years ago. My dad died three days after his fiftieth birthday. We'd thrown a big party for him. I'd give anything if we could have thrown another one for him this year, for his fifty-fifth."

Her voice faded and once again silence engulfed them. Tightening her grip around her legs, she stared into the fire.

"I know it's totally inadequate," Brett said softly, "but I'm real sorry about your dad."

She turned her head and looked at him. He stared straight ahead, his profile cast in flickering shadows from the fire. "Thank you. I appreciate not only the words, but how kind you've been tonight."

He turned to look at her, and when their eyes met, warmth flared through her as if he'd tossed a few more logs on the fire. "You know, I've never lost anyone I've loved."

"You're very fortunate."

"I can't pretend to understand how terrible it is in reality, but based on how the mere thought of losing one of my parents in such an awful way makes me feel…" He shook his head. "I can only say again that I'm sorry for your loss."

"It was bad for all of us, but hardest on my mom. She and Dad met in a public-speaking class their last semester of college. They fell in love like that—" she snapped her fingers "—and married a month after graduation. They were always holding hands and laughing together, and still very much in love. My sisters and I lost our dad, but she lost her best friend, her soul mate and the man she'd planned to spend the rest of her life with. It's taken her a long time to start living again."

A half smile tugged up one corner of her mouth. "Which is why I try not to complain about her matchmaking—fixing me up on dates is sort of like her hobby, but really, I wish she'd try something else. Like stamp-collecting. She's just *bad* at matchmaking. You wouldn't believe some of the men she's introduced me to. It's like a hall of fame for Men No Sane Woman Would Want to Date."

"Does *she* date?"

"She's just starting to dip her toe back in the social pool, which is nice to see. I'm hoping that she'll turn all her matchmaking attention toward finding dating prospects for herself. She's sort of freaked right now about being a grandmother, but a huge part of that is because my dad's not here to be a grandparent with her. I know she's going to take one look at the baby and be a total goner."

"You mentioned you were looking forward to being an aunt."

"Oh, yeah. I was almost ten when my sister Cindy was born. I remember the first time I saw her. Me and Meg and our dad stood at the window at the hospital nursery and Dad pointed Cindy out. It took me exactly half a second to fall in love."

"How about Meg?"

Kayla huffed out a laugh. "It took her a little longer to warm up to our new baby sister. She was thirteen and mortally afraid she'd have to spend her prime teenage dating nights babysitting. I believe her exact first words about Cindy were 'She's red and wrinkly and Kayla can babysit.'"

He chuckled. "And did you babysit?"

"Heck yes. Every chance I got. My mom did medical transcriptions and worked from home, so she was there to keep a parental eye on things, but it was my job to watch Cindy after school until dinnertime. I loved doing it and my mom paid me." She breathed out a sigh, noting the vapor her breath made in the chilly air. "Now that's what I call a great job—getting paid to do something you love."

"That is definitely the best-case scenario."

His voice held a note of…something that prompted her to ask, "Do you love your job?"

A frown puckered his brow and he didn't answer right away. Finally he said, "I love the research, the challenge to discover something new, the knowledge that it could happen in the next hour or day, having a state-of-the-art laboratory at my disposal. But I hate the political bull crap. A lab is no different than an office as far as needing hip boots to wade through the piles of stink.

"I really enjoy the class I teach at Columbia. I like interacting with the students and faculty. At the lab, I spend most of my time alone, so I especially enjoy my time in the classroom."

His gaze searched hers for several seconds, then he said, "I get tired of being alone."

The quiet words grabbed her. She knew exactly what "alone" felt like, and she didn't like it. "What about your breakthrough discovery? I thought it had made you the toast of the town." Guilt slapped her at the question, but she beat it back, rationalizing that she was asking out of personal curiosity, not in an attempt to gain information for La Fleur.

"Oh yeah. On the surface I'm 'the guy.'" There was no missing the bitter tinge in his voice. "But all that's actually done is isolate me more because I have only myself and a very small group of people I trust to count on to make the right decisions."

She nodded slowly, understanding completely. "So now you've discovered how it feels to be lonely in a crowd."

"I have." His eyes remained steady on hers. "That sounds like the voice of experience talking."

"I suppose it is. And I certainly know what you mean about office politics. Where I work, it not only involves wading through the bull crap, but watching out for the back-stabbers. I envy you having a teaching career you could fall back on. If I had an option, I'd seriously consider leaving."

She'd never said the words out loud before, but the instant she voiced them, she realized how true they were. "I'm tired of placating spoiled divas, of putting a good spin on selfish behavior." *Of being asked to spy on scientists.*

A chill ran through her at the thought, and she shivered.

"Cold?" he asked.

"Sort of." Guilt provided very little warmth.

"Would you like me to get you a blanket? Or I'd be glad to offer some body warmth." He uncrossed his ankles, spread his legs, then bent his knees, creating an inviting cocoon for her.

Since body warmth sounded much nicer than a blanket, she resettled herself between his thighs, resting her back against his broad chest. His arms came around her, encircling her with heat, his hands resting atop hers. He smelled clean, like the soap she'd brought to the river, and an image of them washing each other, touching each other, flashed through her mind, instantly evaporating any lingering chill.

"Better?" he asked, his warm breath whispering across her cheek.

"Yes." In fact, it was downright scary how much better. "Thank you."

"My pleasure. Men naturally generate more body heat than women. No point in letting it go to waste."

"No, indeed." Her eyes slid closed and she snuggled closer to his masculine warmth. The press of his legs surrounding hers, his strong arms wrapped around her, the wall of his chest behind her…it was like being wrapped in a Brett-scented blanket.

"So tell me," he said, the stubble on his chin brushing against her hair, "who are these divas you do PR for—a bunch of teenage movie stars?"

"Almost as bad. A bunch of drama-prone models famous for behaving badly, and the drama-prone photographers who take pictures of them."

"Ugh. The lab is looking better and better. How long have you been at your job?"

"Ten years. I was promoted to director of public relations last year. At first I was thrilled, and up until then I had really loved my job. But now…now I'm just…tired. Burned out, I guess."

"Out of balance."

"Exactly."

"Have you looked for another job?"

She shook her head and her temple bumped against his jaw. "I've invested ten years there."

"But if you're really not happy, maybe you should consider going elsewhere. Remember what the *No Change, No Gain* article stated about jobs—that the workplace is where we spend one-third of our adult life. That's a lot of time to be unhappy, so if your job is compromising your core happiness, it's time to consider a change."

She tipped her head back to look at him. "Did you memorize the article?"

"Not word for word, but I've read it enough times to remember it well."

"Have you considered leaving your job?"

"No. But the decisions I make regarding my breakthrough will impact my future and my career. So changes are looming on the horizon."

The word *breakthrough* elicited another frisson of guilt. "I hope that whatever those changes are, they're happy ones," she said softly, meaning every word.

"Thanks. Me, too. Right now I feel like I'm swimming through shark-infested waters with the shore nowhere in sight." His arms tightened briefly. "Well, not right *now.* Right now I'm feeling warm and relaxed and happy."

Pow—another guilt pie in the face. Little did he know that he was embracing one of the very sharks he'd flown to South America to escape. The knowledge tightened her stomach into an aching knot.

"I'm feeling the same way," she said, again meaning every word. "And grateful. For you keeping me company. And listening. And making me laugh."

His shoulders lifted in a shrug. "It was purely selfish on my part. I like hearing you laugh."

She shook her head. "You're trying to make light of what you did, but I won't let you. It was very nice of you."

"I'm a nice guy." She felt him smile against her temple. "Ask my mom. She'll tell you."

"I don't need to ask her. I can tell." Her heart squeezed. Figured—first nice man she'd met in months and their relationship was doomed to end in only a few days. Jeez. If she didn't have rotten, stinking luck, she wouldn't have any luck at all.

"You looked like you needed a friend," he said softly against her ear, shooting pleasurable tingles down her spine. "I'm glad I was here."

"Me, too." She squeezed her eyes shut, refusing to acknowledge how it hurt that she liked him so much and her duplicity had destroyed any chance they might have had of taking their friendship further.

16

"TIME TO wake up, everyone! Breakfast in twenty minutes."

Paolo's cheerful voice drifted through the closed tent flap and Brett slowly came awake, wincing at the stiffness in his back. The problem with sleeping on the damn ground was that when you awoke, you felt as if you'd slept on the damn ground.

But then something warm and soft and fragrant moved against him, and his discomfort evaporated like water in a desert.

Kayla.

He breathed deeply and the luscious, clean scent of her filled his head. She lay next to him, on her side, her cheek pillowed against his shoulder, one slim hand resting on his chest, one leg nestled between his thighs.

His arms tightened around her, absorbing the sensation of her pressed against him. Of waking up with her in his arms after sleeping together.

And only sleeping.

When the fire had died down to nothing but glowing embers, leaving the air around them cold, he'd risen, then helped her to her feet. Shadows of exhaustion had shaded violet circles under her eyes, and without a word, he'd taken her hand and led her to his tent. After helping her remove her coat and boots, he'd removed his own, then they'd slipped into his sleeping bag. She'd instantly snuggled close to him, and seconds later her deep, even breathing indicated she'd fallen asleep. He'd gently kissed the top of her head, and joined her in slumber.

Now she stirred in his arms, and a wave of contentment such as he'd never known rolled through him like warm honey coursing through his veins. They were fully clothed, hadn't shared so much as a kiss last night, yet he felt profoundly satisfied.

In spite of last night's lack of lovemaking, they'd still shared something very intimate and special. He wasn't sure what name to assign to an evening such as the one they'd spent, but he knew the end result was that he felt closer to her than to any woman who'd come before her.

And it was getting damn difficult to imagine another woman coming after her.

She stirred again then raised her head and blinked. Red curls were flattened where she'd pillowed her head against him, and on the other side, they sprang wildly up like miniature corkscrews. Lids still heavy with sleep half covered her eyes, but he was relieved to note the dark smudges beneath them were gone. She looked rumpled and adorable and sexy as hell.

Their gazes met and a slight smile curved her full lips.

"Hi," she murmured in a sleep-roughened voice.

One word. One look. That's all it took and he felt turned inside out. Brett brushed back her hair, his hand lingering over her velvety cheek.

"Hi," he managed to say.

He shifted onto his side, urging her onto her back,

then lowered his head, sinking slowly into a deep, lush, openmouthed kiss. It felt like a reacquaintance after a long absence, a languid exploration of lips and tongues, a leisurely build of arousal.

With that same wordless lack of haste, gazes clinging, they removed their clothes. Brett slid a condom from his backpack, and after rolling on the protection, settled himself between her splayed thighs.

He entered her slowly, shuddering at the silken glide into her wet heat. He stilled for several long seconds, absorbing the satin pleasure of her grip. Then he slowly withdrew, sank deep again, watching every nuance pass over her features, concentrating on breathing in tandem with her slow, deep breaths.

Her breathing grew more rapid and he increased the pace and depth of his strokes to match the tempo. A flushed sheen colored her skin, and her eyes glazed and darkened with need. Wrapping her legs around his waist, she pulled his mouth to hers for another deep, intimate kiss. When she arched beneath him, he swallowed her low groans, letting himself go at the first pulsing squeeze of her orgasm.

Still buried in her slick heat, heart still pounding, he lifted his head. And found her looking up at him through green eyes still hazy with arousal. And knew in that moment that there was no better place on the entire damn planet than this—stretched out over her warm, soft body.

He wanted to say something lighthearted, toss out some quick-witted quip, but he had nothing. A veritable beehive of unfamiliar feelings buzzed through him, but not one of them could be described as lighthearted.

She reached up and traced her fingertips over his face, as if trying to memorize his features. "What am I going to do," she whispered, "when friends ask me what my favorite part of this trip was? How can I tell them that even amidst all this history and scenic beauty, my favorite part was falling asleep in your arms? Waking up wrapped around you? Soft, slow, morning sex with you?"

He had to swallow to find his voice. "I don't know. When you figure it out, pass it along, because I'll need to know what to tell my friends when they ask me that question."

A tiny frown creased her brow. "Thank you," she said softly. "For last night. For holding me and keeping me warm and…being my friend."

He touched his forehead to hers. "Thank you for letting me help. It felt good to be needed."

The sound of muffled voices drifted in through the tent flap. Brett raised his head and sniffed. "Hey. I smell bacon. And coffee."

She raised her head and sniffed, then her eyes widened. "Me, too." She shot him a devilish grin. "Bet I can get dressed and make it to the bacon and coffee before you can."

"A princess like you?" he said with an exaggerated scoff. "I don't *think* so. Especially seeing as how you're on the bottom."

"I won't be as soon as you reach for your clothes."

"You're dealing with a man who really likes bacon. And really needs a cup of coffee."

"You're dealing with a woman who *really* likes bacon and who *really* needs a cup of coffee. Care to place a wager?"

"I'm not normally a gambling man, but hell, this is like shooting fish in a barrel. What are you willing to lose?"

"What do you want?"

You. The word jumped into his mind, reverberating through him. Since the answer was so glaringly clear, he said it out loud. "You."

"Ah. A flesh payment."

"Correct."

"And if *I* win, oh great professor of chemistry, what are *you* willing to lose?"

He shot her a slow grin. "I'm not going to lose."

"Humor me."

"Okay, princess. What do you want?"

"You." Her eyes filled with mischief. "Twice."

"You realize that's a win-win for me. Literally."

"Never let it be said that I'm not willing to share the prize."

"And if I refuse your wicked demands?"

"Then I won't let you have any of my bacon after I get to the kitchen tent first."

"You're very confident for a woman who's going to get left in the dust."

"You're very confident for a man who's going to have to pleasure me for hours—in the method of my choosing."

He raised his brows and nodded approvingly. "Dealer's choice?"

"Absolutely. Any complaints?"

"Hell, no."

She smiled up into his eyes, and his heart executed that crazy acrobatic maneuver it had taken to performing every time she looked at him.

"May the best man win," he said.

"May the best *woman* win," she corrected. "Ready?"

"Ready."

"On your mark, get set, go!"

17

"YOU TOTALLY cheated."

Brett's words, uttered softly so only she could hear them, had Kayla biting back a smile. The group had just departed the campsite, falling into pairs as they made their way along the trail which, according to Paolo, would soon begin to climb.

Arranging her face into a mask of innocence, she turned toward him. In spite of his grumpy tone, his golden-brown eyes glowed with teasing warmth. She lifted her chin and said in her haughtiest voice, "Cheat? I did no such thing."

"Did, too. When you made the wager, your exact words were, 'Bet I can *get dressed* and make it to the bacon and coffee before you can.' The only reason you won was because you didn't bother to get dressed before you hauled ass to the kitchen tent."

"Not true. I was dressed. Did you see me haul my *naked* ass to the kitchen tent? No, you did not."

"A technicality—although I have to admit that's a sight I wouldn't say no to seeing. And now you're cheating again—trying to distract me by mentioning your naked ass."

She batted her eyelashes. "Is it working?"

"Yes. So cut it out."

"You know, you're really cute when you're all frowning and fierce."

His lips twitched, but he recovered quickly and glowered at her. "Stop that. The point is you led me to believe that we had to get dressed. You dashing out of the tent wearing only my flannel shirt does *not* constitute getting dressed."

"I disagree. All my pertinent parts were covered."

"Barely." His scowl deepened. "I thought Miguel's and Alberto's eyeballs were going to pop out on springs—right after they picked up their jaws from the ground."

As much as she was ashamed to admit it, she couldn't deny the feminine thrill that curled through her at the jealousy in his disgruntled tone.

"Don't be silly. They didn't say a word about it."

"That's because they took one look at you, all sexy and tousled and bare-legged and *sexy,* and swallowed their tongues."

A bubble of laughter tickled her throat. "Good grief, I wear less at the beach."

A low groan passed his lips. "Which makes me wish we were at the beach."

That makes two of us, Mr. I Want to Get My Life Back in Balance so I'm Gonna Take a Freakin' Four-Day Hike in the Freakin' Mountains Where Freakin' Bathrooms Don't Exist. "You're just upset that *you* didn't think of not putting on all your clothes before leaving the tent."

"And do you know why I didn't think of that?" Before she could answer, he leaned closer and said in a stage whisper, "Because *I'm* not a cheater."

She raised her chin, refusing to acknowledge the warmth that spread through her when their shoulders bumped. "There's a difference between cheating and finding a legitimate loophole."

He snorted. "Legitimate loophole...that's an oxymoron if I've ever heard one."

"The problem is that you're looking at this with a glass-half-empty mindset. Instead, you should be thanking me for my ingenuity."

"How do you figure?"

"Jeez. For a guy with a Ph.D., you sure are slow to grasp the salient point. If you'd won, I'd owe you *one* flesh payment. Because I won, you owe me *two*." She inched up her chin another notch. "I think I'm insulted that you're complaining."

"Oh, I'm not complaining. And I'm not failing to grasp anything. I had no intention of making it to the kitchen before you. I would have spent half an hour tying my boots if necessary to insure you left the tent first."

She stared at him, nonplussed, then sputtered, "You mean you *let* me win?"

"With *two* flesh payments on the line? Hell, yes."

"But...but that's cheating!"

He laughed. "Now that's like rubidium calling cesium an alkali metal."

She narrowed her eyes. "Okay, I don't know what that means, Mr. Science, but I'm guessing it's along the lines of a dog calling a cat hairy."

"Exactly." He waggled his brows. "And thanks to my delaying tactics, I'll not only get lucky *twice,* I also got to enjoy the view of you all bent-over and pantyless while you struggled to get out of the tent before me. Gotta tell ya, Kayla, it was one hell of a fabulous sight."

"Humph. I think I'm mad at you."

"Great. I'll get make-up sex, too. And then there's also the matter of that erotic massage someone we both know mentioned." A positively wicked grin curved his lips. "Wow. This is the best four-day hike *ever.*"

It was nearly impossible to keep a straight face, but she tried. "You are completely incorrigible."

He shrugged. "Sticks and stones and all that jazz. Now you've merely given me more incentive to inspire you to find other, more complimentary, words to describe me."

"What makes you think I'll come up with anything more complimentary than *incorrigible?*"

His gaze wandered down her body, the blatantly lustful fire in his eyes sending a surge of heat right into her socks. By the time his gaze settled again on hers, she felt as if she'd been roasted over a barbecue spit. "Based on me losing our wager, I have at least two opportunities to inspire you," he said in a low, compelling voice. "And I intend to do so."

Good grief, they must have hiked significantly closer to the sun because it was *hot* out here. The thought of all the delicious things he'd do to her so thoroughly hazed over her brain receptors, Kayla had to shake her head to clear away the lust-induced fuzz. "Looking forward to that."

An understatement if she'd ever uttered one.

"Good." He shot her a wink, then a slight frown formed between his brows. "You said something about me having a Ph.D. How did you know that?"

Her footsteps faltered and her breathing stuttered at the instant realization she'd made a mistake—because he'd never mentioned having a Ph.D. She knew he'd earned his doctorate because of the file La Fleur had compiled on him. Guilt nearly strangled her, warring with a sense of relief that he might figure out the truth and she'd be finished with her distasteful mission.

Still, her promise to Nelson weighed heavily on her mind. Didn't she owe it to him, if not actually to spy on Brett, then at least not to screw up La Fleur's chances of winning his formula? Yes, she supposed she did. And then there was the matter of the bonus, perks and promotion Nelson had hinted at—very tempting in spite of herself. But she liked this less and less. And herself less and less right along with it.

She forced a smile and hoped she didn't look the way she felt—like a deer caught in the headlights. "You must have mentioned it." *Ouch.* Her conscience slapped her hard for that one and she barely managed not to wince at the blow.

"I didn't. I rarely mention credentials unless I'm specifically asked. Otherwise it sounds like I'm pushing an agenda or showing off."

"Oh." Jeez, could she feel any worse? The man was not only a genius, he was modest, too. "I guess I just assumed, what with you teaching a class at Columbia and all. I wouldn't think such a prestigious university would hire anything less than the best and brightest to teach all those brilliant students."

She was saved from finding a way to change the subject when Paolo halted the group. "The trail will become steeper and more rugged from here and you'll notice our current sub-tropical vegetation, which is quite dense, changing as we gain altitude. The next ruins are at Llullucharoc, about an hour's steep climb. I caution you all to watch your step and regulate your breathing. Keeping conversation to a minimum will help, although feel free to speak if you feel capable. If anyone needs to slow down or stop, please signal me." He flashed his bright smile. "We do not want any casualties on the trail."

Everyone fell back into line and Kayla pressed her hand to her jittery midsection. "Casualties?" she whispered to Brett. "Jeez, that Paolo. He's a laugh a minute."

He chuckled and reached out to squeeze her hand. "You have a last will and testament, right?"

"Oh, you're hysterical, too. Really. You and Paolo should take your comedy tour on the road." Even as she said it, she was damn glad she *did* have a last will and testament.

Following Paolo's instructions—because she had no intention of becoming a hike casualty—she focused on the trail and her breathing. The terrain was indeed rough and steep, and her lungs and legs burned with the strenuous uphill climb, none of which was helped by the ever-thinning air and the load of crap she lugged on her back.

By God, if she was ever insane enough to do something like this again—not that she ever would, but just in case a rock hit her in the head and she became that insane by mistake, she would make damn sure she packed less crap. If she was going to lug anything heavy up another mountain, it would have Porta Potti written on its side.

That was, of course, assuming that she survived *this* excursion up the mountain.

After arriving at the ruins, they stopped for a much-needed drink, protein-energy bar, and picture-taking break.

They then prepared to continue on toward the next stop, Llulluchapampa, an isolated village in a flat meadow.

"This next leg of our journey is approximately a two-hour climb, after which we will stop for lunch," Paolo said as they left the ruins. "It is strenuous, but the cloud forest and extraordinary valley views make it well worth the effort."

"You holding up okay?" Brett asked, shrugging his backpack onto his broad shoulders.

"Not too bad. I feel better since I ate something."

"Me, too."

"It's weird, but just when I start to think 'What the hell am I doing here?' we see something else amazing. Another species of orchid or bird or these latest ruins, and it hits me what an incredible experience this is." She rolled her sore shoulders and grimaced at the deep ache radiating down her back. "Of course there have also been plenty of moments when I've thought I'd be just as happy, if not happier, looking at pictures of this place while in the comfort of my own bathroom-equipped apartment."

The hike resumed, and Paolo had not exaggerated about the difficulty of the climb. There was little conversation, for which she was grateful, as ignoring the growing ache in her legs and back required all her concentration. Yet, as hard as the going was, the sights were astounding. They literally walked through clouds, fingers of white vapor brushing over them, dissipating as they passed.

The views of the verdant valley and churning river

below brought exclamations of wonder, and camera shutters clicked at regular intervals. When they finally stopped for lunch, the entire group released a collective groan of relief. Kayla shrugged off her backpack, letting it fall to the ground with a dull thud. She then plopped down beside it, closed her eyes and groaned.

She felt the thud of Brett's backpack landing next to hers. Heard his long release of breath as he sat next to her. Felt his hand settle on hers.

"I used to think my yoga and spinning classes were brutal," she murmured, "but those last two hours really kicked my ass. I think I need a transfusion."

"Well, if it's any consolation, princess, *everyone's* ass is kicked."

She peeked her eyes open and noticed that all the other hikers were also sprawled on the ground. It offered little comfort that Ashley, who was probably a good ten years younger than her, looked as wrung-out as Kayla felt. They exchanged weak smiles, then Kayla's gaze fell upon their guide.

"Everyone's ass is kicked except Paolo's. And his siblings." She regarded the four Trucero siblings with a baleful, yet grudgingly respectful look. "They all appear fresh and energetic and probably could have *sprinted* up the damn trail."

"They're used to the altitude."

"Right. It's solely the altitude that has my thighs screaming and my back weeping."

"Well, that's my excuse. And I'm sticking to it."

After a simple but delicious lunch of ham and cheese sandwiches, the group started out once again. Before picking up her backpack, Kayla rubbed her lower back and shot the heavy load of crap—as she not so affectionately called it—a dirty look.

"If all this damn hiking doesn't make my ass smaller, I'm going to write a very strongly worded letter of complaint to the Inca Trail authorities."

"There is nothing wrong with your ass," Brett assured her.

"Right. Except that it feels like it's dragging on the ground. And, according to Paolo, aka Mr. Susie Sunshine, we haven't yet even hit the most difficult part of the day's hike."

"We're now about to embark on the most rigorous and punishing segment of our journey," said Mr. Susie Sunshine, and Kayla barely managed not to groan. Rigorous and punishing. Sooo not the two words her already abused muscles wanted to hear.

"The terrain will change from light woodland to scrub, and then to grassland and bare slope, growing ever more rugged until we reach the highest point on the trail at nearly fourteen thousand feet, Abra de Huarmihuanusqa, or Dead Woman's Pass. The origin of the name is unknown."

"Seems self-explanatory to me," Kayla said, in an undertone to Brett. "Unfortunately."

They started off and Kayla quickly realized that *punishing and rigorous* were understatements. She would have used *torturous and grueling*. The going was slow, the thin air forcing numerous thirty-second breaks. The sun scorched down in brutal, relentless rays, baking them, only for the weather to abruptly change to freezing winds as they neared the summit.

She might have voiced her misery out loud, but she

simply didn't have the energy or lung power to do so. All her efforts and strength were required to keep putting one foot in front of the other.

Yet, despite the harshly exhausting conditions, everyone in the group took comfort in that they were all in this together. Clearly misery did love company, and it made it easier to bear the hardship knowing she wasn't alone.

When they finally reached the summit, the bedraggled, exhausted hikers all exchanged hugs and high fives. After a well-deserved rest complete with another light snack, they readied themselves to begin the steep descent into the valley toward Pacamayo, where they'd camp for the night.

Kayla took one last look back at the trail from which they'd comc. "Ncvcr in my life have I done anything that draining or intense," she told Brett.

"Same here. I'm proud of you, princess. I didn't hear a single complaint."

"Who had air to spare to complain? And I'm proud of you, too. Of all of us. Including myself. When I get home, I'm going to have a custom T-shirt made—I hiked to Dead Woman's Pass and it didn't kill me. At least not completely."

Any hope she'd harbored that the descent into the valley would be less strenuous evaporated within minutes. The path descended sharply, on uneven, complicated stone steps that required close concentration. The only part that was noticeably easier was that the air became a bit less thin as they approached the valley.

By the time they arrived in Pacamayo, they'd hiked nearly seven miles—about the same distance as the day before. But today's journey felt like seventy miles in comparison.

When they finally stopped, Kayla shrugged off her backpack, allowing it simply to thump to the ground. She instantly followed suit then curled into a fetal position and whimpered, "I am one with the dirt. Go on without me. Save yourself."

She heard Brett chuckle, then hiss out a curse. "Please, do not make me laugh." A long, deep groan followed, and she pried open one eye and watched him lower himself to the ground next to her. Using his backpack as a back rest, he reached out and plucked up her limp form with an ease that majorly impressed her. She couldn't have plucked up so much as a daisy if her life had depended on it. He settled her in his lap, and she curled against him, her head flopping like a rag doll's on his chest.

"Why aren't you half-dead like me?" she asked.

"I'm pretty tired."

"*Pretty tired?* I left 'pretty tired' behind about six miles ago. I don't want to be a whiner, but my God, *everything* hurts. My *hair* hurts. My *eyebrows* hurt. Even my earlobes hurt. Parts of me I didn't even know I had ache. There is not one bit of balance in my life—only profound soreness. Whose crazy idea was this anyway?" A moan escaped her. "I knew I should have gone to the Caribbean to find my balance. No change, no gain? What a pile of pain-filled hooey."

His chuckle shook his chest. "Poor princess. You've really been a trooper. I haven't heard a complaint all day. Of course, you're making up for it now, but since everybody's lying on the ground in various stages of moaning and groaning, I won't hold it against you. And lucky for you, I know just the thing to make you feel better."

"You have a morphine drip handy?"

"'Fraid not. But I do have what you need."

"I'd ask what that is, but I'm too busy trying to remember how to say 'Where's the hospital?' in Spanish."

"As luck would have it, I'm a doctor. And I give excellent physical therapy."

"You're not a medical doctor, and the only thing I'm physically capable of right now is…nothing. Okay, here's a sentence I never thought I'd say, especially to an exceptionally hot and willing guy—I'm too tired for sex."

"Compliment of 'exceptionally hot' noted and appreciated. But I wasn't talking about sex. I was talking about a back rub. After I'm done, you'll feel brand-new."

"Brand-new would be nice. Because old, battered, aching, creaky and sore really sucks."

"Fear not. I'll rub away all your aches and pains."

"Gotta warn ya, you'll be rubbing for a really long time."

His lips brushed against her temple, warm and comforting. "A really long time," he repeated softly. "That's what I'm counting on, princess."

18

"HOW DOES THAT FEEL, princess?"

Ensconced in his small tent, Brett smiled at the long pleasure-filled sigh that constituted Kayla's response. He continued to smooth his hands down her bare back, alternating long, gliding strokes with a circular kneading motion, working out the soreness and kinks.

He felt surprisingly well, considering the brutal workout of today's hike. Of course, the warm shower after a hearty dinner had helped considerably toward reviving him. Not that there were any facilities here, other than the same bathroom-tent set-up as last night. But tonight, instead of "showering" with ice-cold river water, Ana had heated large pots of water so that everyone had gotten a bucket of warm water with which to bathe away the day's dirt and sweat and strain.

A combination of pity and amusement curved his lips as he recalled how piteously grateful Kayla had been for the steaming water, with Eileen and Ashley not far behind in their gratitude. The men had been just as grateful—just less gushy than the ladies.

As he had last night, Alberto had directed them to a private area where they stripped. He'd held up Kayla's bucket for her, tilting it to produce a thin stream of warm water under which she gratefully soaped up and rinsed. The air was chilled with a brisk breeze and they hadn't lingered, just washed and dressed in clean clothes, then made their way back to the campsite.

The tents had been set up while they showered, and after dinner they'd bade the other hikers—all of whom were dragging their tired butts to their own tents—good night.

Once he and Kayla were inside his tent, Brett had secured the flap. Space was tight, but he had no objection to sharing a cozy space with her. She'd flopped facedown onto his sleeping bag and expelled a long moan.

"I may never move again," she'd whispered.

"You don't have to. Just relax."

"Relax. Okay, good thing you told me that 'cause otherwise I would have hopped up and jogged a few miles."

Chuckling softly, he'd stripped her of her clothes, then removed his T-shirt, but kept on his sweat pants. Straddling the backs of her thighs, he'd asked, "Do you have any sort of lotion in your backpack?"

"Front zipper compartment. Unscented stuff, so as not to attract bugs or snakes or whatever other creepy crawlers might be slithering about."

"Good thinking."

He'd located a tube bearing the La Fleur symbol and after squeezing some into his hand, rubbed his palms together to warm the lotion, then started slowly massaging his way down her back.

Now, twenty minutes later, she was showing small signs of life.

"That feels sooo goood," she said as he worked out

the tight knots in her shoulders. "If I'm ever able to rise from this spot, I swear I'll pay you back."

"Looking forward to that. But I'm fine. Let's just focus on getting you whipped back into shape."

"Okay. I'll give you three days to quit massaging me. Not a minute more. Really. If you haven't stopped by then, I'll have to call the cops."

"I'm not too worried. You don't know how to call the cops in Spanish."

"Oh. Right. So I guess you'll just have to stop on your own after the three days are up."

"Deal."

"Have I told you what a nice man you are?"

"Twice. But hey, I like hearing it, so feel free."

"You're a very nice man."

"Thank you."

"Who has very nice, very talented hands."

"Uh-huh. Keep going."

"Trolling for compliments?"

"Let's just say I'd be willing to listen to any flattery you might want to toss my way."

"You're very smart. And strong. And thanks to you and the shower you gave me and this incredible massage, I may actually be able to move in the morning."

"My pleasure." His hands slowly rubbed their way down toward the base of her spine. "Anything else?"

One green eye peeked at him over her shoulder. "You mean other than sexy and witty and sexy and gorgeous and sexy?" She resettled her head against her folded arms. "Nah, I think that about covers everything."

"You're very nice, too, you know."

For several seconds she stiffened under his hands. "I...I'm glad you think so."

"I do. And you know that whole sexy, witty, sexy, gorgeous, sexy thing you said about me? Well, same goes, princess."

And speaking of gorgeous and sexy...his gaze followed his hands' path down the smooth, pale skin on her back, pausing over several scatterings of gilt freckles, skimming lower, until he gently kneaded her rounded buttocks. A prolonged *mmm* escaped her and she lifted her butt into his touch. Given the spectacular view, he was already as hard as steel, but his body reacted immediately, tightening further at her movement. He hadn't really considered what sweet torture this massage would be for him.

Forcing himself to put aside his growing need and continue his ministrations, he shifted, nudging her thighs apart, then resettled himself on his knees between her spread legs. Squeezing out another generous dollop of lotion, he massaged her hips, then made his way down each shapely leg, manipulating the backs of her thighs and calves. Her long, soft moans of approval told him he was hitting all the right spots.

"Feel good?" he asked, working the arch of her foot with strong sweeping strokes of his thumbs.

"*Good* doesn't begin to describe it. I think my toes just had an orgasm."

The word *orgasm* shot arrows of pure lust through him, and he inhaled sharply. And caught the subtle scent of female arousal. Apparently she was as turned on as him. *Thank God.*

Sitting on his heels, he worked his way back up her legs. When he reached her buttocks, he changed the speed and strength of his strokes from healing massage to sensual caress. He spread his knees more, opening her thighs wider. His fingers lightly kneaded her supple flesh, then dipped lower.

Her sex was wet and soft, and he stroked two fingers into the velvety heat, while his other hand continued to gently massage her bottom.

"Brett..." His name was a husky groan filled with want, and his body responded by tightening to the point of pain. With another groan, she lifted herself up onto her elbows and pushed back against his hand.

"More," she rasped, panting. "More."

He added a third finger, pumping slowly. Her breathing turned more ragged and finally, with a strangled *aaahhhh,* her slick walls pulsed around him.

When her ripples subsided, he slipped out his fingers. Instead of going totally limp as he'd expected her to, she instead pushed herself up on her knees, then looked at him over her shoulder. Her eyes glittered with enough heat to incinerate him.

"More."

The husky command was one he was more than happy—and beyond ready—to obey. He pulled a condom from the front pocket of his backpack and gave thanks that his sweatpants made for easy access. He pushed down the soft material and his boxers to his hips. His erection sprang free and he quickly sheathed himself. With his butt resting on his heels, he grasped her waist and positioned her wet opening over the head of his penis.

She slid down slowly, her sleek inner walls gripping him like a heated fist. When he was fully engulfed, her back pressed against his chest, he leaned forward and scraped his teeth across her shoulder, lightly biting her smooth skin, then fastened his mouth on the sensitive skin of her nape. A shudder ran through her.

"More," she whispered, putting her hands over his, sliding them up her torso until his closed over her breasts.

His fingers played with her hard nipples, teasing, tugging, as he thrust upward, his movements measured and deliberate in an effort to hold off coming as long as possible. But she wasn't helping him retain his control. She slowly circled her hips in such a mind-blowing way he saw stars. Urgent, brutal need churned through him. He wasn't going to last much longer.

Cruising one hand downward, he curved his fingers over her mound and caressed her wet flesh. He thrust harder, faster, gritting his teeth, holding off coming by sheer will. The instant he felt the first ripple of her orgasm, he clamped his arm around her waist, surging up while urging her down, imbedding himself deeper and letting go.

They were both still breathing hard when she leaned back fully against him, and pressed her lips to the side of his neck where his pulse throbbed.

He closed his eyes and bent his head to breathe her in, her own unique scent mixed with the heady musk of her arousal.

"Wow," she whispered.

"My favorite scientific term. More?"

He felt her smile against his neck. "That's enough—for now. Check back in five, ten minutes."

That's enough.

His insides jittered at the words, instantly rejecting

them. No, it wasn't enough. And he couldn't imagine it ever being enough. Not just the sex—which was inarguably outstanding—but everything to do with this woman. Her laugh, her humor, her determination to keep herself together on the trail today. The way she made him feel just by standing next to him.

She'd grabbed his attention from the first instant he'd seen her, and that fascination, that instant chemistry he'd experienced, hadn't waned one bit. It had only grown stronger. Along with his feelings.

The realization ripped through him with the intensity of an atomic explosion.

He was falling in love with her.

Falling? his inner voice interjected. *Who the hell do you think you're kidding? You're way beyond falling. You're splattered all over the ground.*

He went perfectly still, unable to deny it. He was in love with Kayla.

Probably that realization should have scared the crap out of him, but instead, a sense of calm settled over him that he'd finally found a woman who could make him feel this way. So what if it had happened fast? There weren't rules about how long it had to take to fall in love. His own parents were a perfect example. This was *right.* Kayla was, unequivocally, "the one."

The words *I love you* involuntarily rushed up from his pounding heart, and he had to press his lips together to keep himself from saying them out loud. They weren't words he said lightly. And he'd never been tempted to utter them to anyone after such a short acquaintance. But then, no woman had ever made him feel the way this woman did.

It was definitely too soon to tell her. She'd not only think he was crazy, he'd probably scare her off. And there was no rush. They lived in the same city. Although they hadn't yet discussed continuing their relationship after the hike, as far as he was concerned, it was a no-brainer. There was absolutely no reason for their adventure to end once they returned home, no long-distance issues to deal with.

That realization suffused him with a profound sense of peace, and he could almost feel the out-of-alignment parts of his life shifting back into balance—like car gears slipping into place.

No, this wasn't enough.

And he intended to see to it that it didn't have to be.

19

THE NEXT morning, Kayla walked carefully along the dirt trail as the group made their way single-file through a narrow pass toward their first stop of the day, the ruins of Runkuracay.

She knew Brett walked directly behind her and was probably ogling her butt—knowledge that should have made her smile, but instead pulled a frown between her brows and added another rock to the heavy weight already pressing upon her heart.

After enjoying a good night's sleep, basking in the luscious sensation of awakening in Brett's arms, a delicious bout of morning sex followed by a scrumptious breakfast, she should have been happy. Yet as many times as she told herself that, she remained troubled. A deepening sense of distress snaked through her, one that grew stronger with each passing hour because each passing hour brought her closer to the time when she and Brett would go their separate ways.

No more waking up in his arms. No more laughter or lopsided grins or enjoying his company or watching his eyes darken with desire for her. No more curling up against him after making love and just listening to his heart beat.

No more Brett.

And that knowledge, the absolute certainty that the end to this magical time with him grew closer with each passing minute, ticked in her mind like a giant, evil clock, mocking her, sneering at her, reminding her that not only would it end, but any feelings he had for her would go the way of the dinosaur.

Because, of course, he'd believe she'd only gotten close to him, slept with him, to gain information for La Fleur, for which she couldn't blame him. How could she? The reality was that she'd followed him to another continent with the sole purpose of spying on him. Of finding out about him and his formula and steering him toward La Fleur. Of dishing out some payback for a perceived wrong. If the situations were reversed, it's certainly what she'd think.

But her mission now left an impossibly bitter taste in her mouth. One that burned like acid every time she swallowed.

Maybe she should just tell him the truth. Hope he'd understand. But why would he? Why should he? No, he'd just toss her aside sooner rather than later and these last couple of days on the trail would turn into a nightmare—one that would continue back in New York after Nelson found out she'd spilled the beans. There'd be no more talk of bonuses, perks, or a promotion. Hell, she'd probably lose her job. Even if Nelson didn't fire her, certainly her work environment would turn uncomfortable.

Bottom line was that regardless of what she did, at the end of this adventure, because of her actions, Brett was lost to her. And that harsh truth filled her with such an aching, profound sense of loss, she could barely catch her breath—in a way that had nothing to do with the thin air.

And on top of that sense of loss was her deep shame at her own actions. When, precisely, had she turned into the sort of person who would spy on someone else? Look through their belongings? Seek revenge, especially for a merely *perceived* wrong, and most especially without finding out all the facts?

She'd always prided herself on her integrity and sense of fair play, yet sometime during this past year, since she'd been promoted to director—and most recently during this past week—she'd become someone she didn't like very much. Someone who was willing to do things she knew in her soul weren't honorable, all in the name of furthering her career.

No, that wasn't a person she liked at all. Not a person Brett would admire if he knew the truth. And he deserved better. Because he was, without a doubt, a decent, good man. A kind and honorable man. The sort of man a woman could envision herself sharing a future with.

A man she could have fallen in love with.

If her actions hadn't doomed them from the start.

Could have fallen? her inner voice asked with a derisive snort. *Don't you mean* have *fallen in love with?*

She rubbed her temple in a vain attempt to stave off the headache the torturous question threatened. Had she fallen in love? God help her, she was so confused she didn't know what she felt anymore, but she greatly feared she had. How foolish could she possibly be?

She barely resisted the urge to thump herself on the head. She'd suffered through this extreme trek with the hopes of regaining some balance in her life, but instead, because of her actions, the fact that she'd fallen for a man she couldn't have, and the added bonus that her conscience was eating her alive, she felt more out of balance now than she ever had before.

And, to add insult to injury, they'd barely begun today's nine and half miles and already every muscle protested. And her hair looked like a rat's nest. And her nose was sunburned. And her back itched. And damn it, she had to pee.

The day was not off to a good start.

An hour later, after viewing the small, circular ruins at Runkuracay, which were thought to be a way post for couriers and stabling facilities for their animals, they continued their strenuous climb toward the top of the second pass, Abra de Runkuracay, then began the steep descent into the valley which contained a shallow, picturesque lake. They enjoyed a light snack, for which the group was especially grateful as the descent had been particularly hard on their tired knees.

When they started off again, Paolo said, "Here the trail changes from dirt path to a narrow stone roadway, which is the original work of the Incas, and the start of the true Inca Trail."

Even though her soul remained troubled, Kayla couldn't deny the sense of wonder that infused her as they walked along the ancient Incas' path. The scenery was particularly breathtaking, with vistas of the mountains and valley below.

While the hike was not as brutally grueling as the previous day's, it was still exhausting, and Kayla was grateful for the numerous stops to view ruins along the way. They climbed, then descended to the Inca ruins at

Sayacmarca—which translated to Town in a Steep Place, a perfect name as far as she was concerned.

Then, more climbing and descending, passing magnificent flora—orchids, tree ferns and hanging mosses—to Phuyupatamarca, or Town in the Clouds, which everyone agreed was the most impressive site so far. The only way to access it was to navigate a steep flight of stone stairs. Leaving the ruins involved a plummeting descent down a flight of over two thousand stone steps. When they reached the bottom, she said to the group, "I'm ready to call in an orthopedic surgeon for an estimate on knee replacement."

Everyone laughingly agreed. "Can't," Paolo said with his bright smile. "No cell service."

She shot him "the look." "Thanks for that reminder."

Her guilt increased throughout the day because of Brett's thoughtful solicitousness. He chatted with her, held her hand, helped her down those stairs from hell, each gesture making her feel like a bigger rat. Unable to stand the self-reproach, on the pretext of asking Paolo a question, she moved to the front of the line, away from Brett, then remained there—but only hated herself even more for the dishonesty of the ploy.

After a hearty lunch of cured ham, mountain cheese and dried fruit, during which she made a point of conversing with the other hikers, they continued for several more hours, walking through ethereal cloudforest until they arrived at Huinay Huayna, named for the gorgeous perpetually blooming pink orchid of the same name. Paolo then announced he had a surprise for them, and led them a short way back along the trail to a tin-roofed building.

It wasn't the most attractive of places, ramshackle and jarringly out of place amongst all the pristine beauty, but when Paolo announced that hot showers and toilets were available inside, a collective cheer went up.

"A *bathroom,* Brett," she said to him, her voice filled with a piteous awe she couldn't control. "An actual *bathroom.* With a *shower.* And *hot water.* Oh, glorious day!"

He cast a dubious look at the rundown building. "I'm thinking it's not going to be like the Ritz Carlton."

"I don't care. I've never been so glad to hear the words *bathroom* and *shower* in my entire life."

"Glad you're happy. Especially since you've seemed sort of...not happy all day." His gaze searched hers. "Is everything okay?"

No. "Yes." At this point, what was one more lie?

He lightly grasped her arm, then led her several steps away from the others. When he looked at her again, there was no mistaking the mixture of concern and confusion in his eyes. "Kayla...did I say something, do something, to upset you?"

She immediately shook her head, then reached out and placed her hand against his whisker-roughened cheek. "No. You've been...perfect."

"But something's wrong. Can I help?"

She briefly squeezed her eyes shut. *Yes. Stop being so nice to me. So wonderful. So generous. So understanding. I'm not the honest person you think I am.*

When she opened her eyes, she drew a deep breath, then said, "Thank you, but as much as I appreciate the offer, I need to work it out on my own." She offered him a weak smile. "I guess all this exposure to nature and peace and quiet has forced me to do some serious self-evaluation, and I've discovered, much to my chagrin, that I've come up short in a few areas."

Comprehension dawned in his eyes. "I'd lay odds that everyone here is in the same boat, myself included. A trip like this offers the time and setting conducive to reflection, which is exactly the change that's needed to gain balance back in our lives." He raised her hand to his lips and kissed her knuckles. "If it's any consolation, I think you're terrific."

To her utter mortification, hot tears pushed behind her eyes. "Thank you. And I think you're...extraordinary." *And, God, I'm going to miss you so much.*

"Thanks." He gave the air an exaggerated sniff then wrinkled his nose. "Of course, I'll think you're even more terrific after you've showered."

Although the facilities were stark and rundown, to Kayla they represented the height of comfort. She luxuriated in her shower, soaping herself twice from head to toe, then dressing in her most comfortable jeans and softest sweatshirt. While the shower hadn't cleansed away any emotional dirt, at least she felt physically clean.

Dinner that night was a gala affair. Ana, Alberto and Miguel had hiked ahead of the group in order to set up the kitchen tent and campsite early. Their meal consisted of *pachamanca,* a classic Inca dish distinguished by its method of underground cooking. Meat, potatoes, cheese, peppers and herbs were baked in a hole in the ground over hot stones, with banana leaves placed between the layers of food.

"The act of cooking in the ground was symbolic for the Incas," Paolo explained while they enjoyed the delicious meal. "Because they worshipped the earth, to eat directly from it was a way of honoring *Pachamama,* Mother Earth, and giving thanks for her bounty."

After dinner, over coffee around the campfire, Paolo said, "On this, the last night of our journey together, I always encourage everyone to talk about the trip thus far—what you've learned, what you think will stick in your minds as memorable years from now when you look back on your hike." He nodded toward Dan Smith, who'd kept mostly to himself over the past two days, and said, "You went last on our first night, *señor,* so I invite you to begin this evening."

Everyone's attention turned to Dan, and as it had the first night, it took him a moment to answer. "This trip has shown me that there are places in the world that go beyond just looking beautiful. These last few days, I've cherished every step, every aching muscle, every extraordinary thing I've seen. I've also missed Marcie so much I could barely breathe. She would have loved this place, but would have *despised* the bathroom tent. Probably even more than Kayla."

His gaze flicked to Kayla who, the entire group agreed, hated the bathroom tent more than anyone else, and the ghost of a smile touched his lips. "My Marcie loved a long soak in the tub."

He cleared his throat. "So I learned I could miss her even more than I thought possible. I learned that it doesn't take long for strangers to feel like family, especially when you're all trying to accomplish the same difficult task."

Again his gaze settled on Kayla and an invisible camaraderie passed between them, squeezing her heart in sympathy for the kindly man. "And I learned that it helps to know other people understand exactly how I feel. Long after the scenery has faded from my memory and I can no longer even see the pictures I've taken, I'll remember how good the accomplishment of this hike, the tranquility of this place and the kindness you people made me feel."

His comments were met with a round of applause. When the clapping died down, Paolo nodded toward Bill and Eileen, indicating they were next.

"Most memorable so far for me," Bill said, "is the way this place has made me think about history. Eileen and I have been to Rome where we spent a day visiting the Forum and the Coliseum and it certainly gave you a sense of ancient times. But you were also surrounded by the very busy, very modern city of Rome. Here, there's nothing but nature for days on end, nothing to pull you out of the past." He winced and rolled his neck. "And based on all my aches and pains, I learned that I'm not as young as I used to be."

"I second that bit about the aches and pains," Eileen said. "Most memorable for me will be the *quiet* of this place. In our hectic, busy lives at home, there's rarely quiet. Between work, our boys, our students, the phone, the doorbell, the television, it's just always so *noisy.* I've really enjoyed the utter stillness and quietness here."

After another round of applause, Paolo pointed to Brett. "How about you, *señor?* Have you found the balance you mentioned seeking on our first night?"

Kayla turned toward Brett, who sat next to her, and stared at his handsome profile. His dark hair gleamed in the golden firelight, and her fingers itched to glide along the tempting plane of his freshly shaved jaw.

"I haven't completely regained my balance because I haven't been able to focus all my energies on deciding what I want to do about my formula." His lips quirked upward. "I've been too busy trying not pass out from lack of oxygen or slide down two thousand stone steps on my butt."

Laughter and nods of commiseration greeted his words. "I've also been a bit preoccupied by a certain beautiful lady," he said, turning to smile at Kayla.

A group "awww" sounded and another knife of guilt stabbed into Kayla's gut.

After shooting her a wink, Brett turned back to the fire. "But in spite of not making the actual decision, my being here, away from the phone and e-mail and craziness, has cleared my mind so that when I return home, I'll be better prepared to make it. Everything else has fallen into place, into balance here, so I'm confident the decision regarding my formula will follow suit. As for what I'll recall as most memorable…"

Again he turned toward Kayla, and the look in his eyes stilled her. Dear God, he was looking at her in a way that made everyone, everything else dissolve. As if no one existed except them. As if she were the most beautiful, desirable woman he'd ever seen.

"I can sum up most memorable in one word," he said softly. With his serious gaze steady on hers, he lifted her hand to his lips and kissed the back of her fingers. "Kayla."

For several long seconds, the only sound was the snapping of the flames while she stared into his beautiful eyes and pretended her heart hadn't twisted into a hard, painful knot. Then someone whistled through their teeth and everyone applauded, jerking her back from the private place where only she and Brett existed. A place where nothing could come between them.

An impossible place that didn't exist.

"That is *so* romantic," Ashley said, giving Shawn an exaggerated jab with her elbow.

"It will be difficult to top what your man said," Paolo told Kayla with a smile.

Your man. The words ricocheted through her, filling her with a dull ache as she realized just how much she wished they were true.

Tears welled in her eyes, and she looked down to hide them. A single droplet plopped on her hand, and she watched it trail over her skin before clearing her throat to rid it of the lump which had lodged there. "This...this has been the single most challenging and fulfilling experience of my life. The *no change, no gain* mantra that brought me here has proven very prophetic. What I think I'll always remember about this adventure is how much I discovered about myself. Some of which I like, some of which I don't."

She blinked back more tears, and in an attempt at lightening a situation that threatened to emotionally crush her, added, "I also learned how much I take the everyday niceties of life—like indoor plumbing—for granted." She then turned and looked at Brett. Their gazes met and her throat closed off. But she couldn't not mention him. "And of course, I'll always remember Brett," she whispered, scarcely able to find her voice. "Brett, who is...unforgettable."

Yes, she'd always remember him—with a deep ache

in her heart for what they'd shared and what might have been if they'd met under different circumstances.

When the applause quieted, Paolo nodded toward Ashley.

"Since I met Shawn, I've taken a lot of camping trips, but this one is, by far, the most strenuous and exhausting. But also the most beautiful. I'll never forget the feeling of pride and accomplishment I experienced when I looked back from Dead Woman's Pass at the trail we'd hiked. And what I've learned is really just a reconfirmation of something I already knew—that I'd rather be exhausted from hiking and living in primitive conditions with Shawn than hanging out at some ritzy resort with anyone else." She leaned over and planted a noisy kiss on his cheek, and the group whooped, whistled and clapped.

After the noise died down, Shawn said, "Well, I'm really glad to hear you say that, babe, because what I've learned on this adventure is really just a reconfirmation of something I already knew—that I never want to be without you. And I'm hoping that the next moment will be our most memorable of this trip." He shifted off the log bench onto one knee, then slipped a small, square box from his pocket. He opened it and a diamond ring sparkled in the firelight.

"Ashley, I knew you were 'the one' the first time I saw you. You're my best friend, my best girl and I love you. Will you marry me?"

Kayla, along with everyone else, silently watched Ashley's eyes widen. Her gaze bounced between Shawn and the ring several times, then, with a sound that was half laugh, half sob, she flung her arms around him and buried her face against his neck.

"I take it that's a yes," Brett leaned over to whisper in Kayla's ear.

"That's my guess," she whispered back.

"Yes!" Shawn shouted, jumping to his feet and dragging Ashley up with him. "She said yes!"

Everyone offered their congratulations to the beaming couple and admired the solitaire ring. Shawn pulled a bottle of champagne from the bottom of his backpack, exclaiming, "This bottle's been burning a hole in my backpack this entire hike."

"Good thing I said yes," Ashley teased, "because now your pack will be considerably lighter."

After pouring some champagne into everyone's coffee mug, Shawn raised his and said, "A toast to my beautiful bride-to-be."

"Who promises to look much more beautiful than I do right now when the big day actually arrives," Ashley added with a happy smile.

After the champagne was finished, and good-nights were said, everyone headed off to get ready for bed. Once Kayla and Brett were ensconced in the intimate coziness of their tent, he remarked, "Nice way to end the evening. Glad she didn't say no. He was pretty nervous."

"How do you know?"

"He told me what he planned to do."

"Really? When?"

"This morning. While we performed that centuries-old male bonding ritual of pissing in the woods. I think he just needed to get it off his chest. And to hear someone tell him he was doing the right thing."

Her brows shot up. "And you told him he was? I

thought the centuries-old male bonding ritual was for men to talk other men out of proposing."

"Maybe some males, but not me. He's crazy in love with her, and even a blind guy can see she's crazy in love with him. I told him to go for it."

He pulled his shirt over his head and she was momentarily distracted by the sight of all those lovely rippling muscles.

She licked her lips then said, "I'm glad it all worked out. And it certainly brought the evening to a memorable end."

Reaching out, he pulled her into his arms and nuzzled her neck with his warm lips. His erection pressed against her belly, shooting heat straight to her core. "I vote we bring the evening to our own memorable end."

"Hmmm. Now *that's* a reason to celebrate."

Yet even as her lips parted for his kiss, heaviness invaded her heart. She knew the celebration would soon be over.

20

WHEN PAOLO'S voice announced it was time to rise and shine, Brett peeked open one eye, deduced from the utter blackness inside the tent that it was still dark outside, groaned and rolled over.

And discovered he was alone.

Hoisting himself up on one elbow, he blinked both eyes open then felt for his flashlight, squinting when its bright glare flooded the tent. The spot beside him was empty. A sight, he realized, he didn't like the look of at all. He shifted the beam of light to his watch and groaned. Three-thirty.

He sniffed the air, catching the enticing aroma of coffee. Since Paolo and Ana were both clearly awake, at least Kayla wasn't alone.

He clicked off the flashlight then flopped onto his back and stacked his hands behind his head, taking a moment to gather his thoughts.

All of which revolved around Kayla.

Specifically around the erotic massage she'd treated him to last night.

Holy hell, it was a miracle the damn tent hadn't gone up in flames. That book she'd read—*Mastering the Art of the Erotic Massage*—well, she'd mastered it, but good.

He closed his eyes and recalled in vivid detail the way she'd removed his clothes, then, using her unscented lotion, first massaged his back, legs and feet with long, gliding strokes, much as he'd massaged her the night before.

But then she'd turned him over and given the same meticulous attention to his chest, arms and hands as she'd lavished on his back, never touching his penis, building an agony of anticipation even as she'd massaged the rest of him into relaxation.

She'd finished by switching her entire focus to his straining erection.

"The basic principle of male genital massage is to build a repeated peaking process," she'd said in a smoky voice. "For me to slow down, stop or change what I'm doing before you come. So let me know when you're about to climax."

And then the sweetest torture he'd ever endured had commenced. She'd cupped him, caressed and teased him, stimulating him over and over with a variety of tempos and strokes that drove him insane. Every time he'd growled out that he was about to explode, she'd switch to something new or sweep her hands up and down the rest of his body until the urgent need to ejaculate subsided. Then she'd begin another slow build.

By the sixth time, his vision had glazed over and he was practically delirious. When he'd grunted that he couldn't take it anymore, she'd leisurely rolled a condom over his aching erection, and proceeded to drive him wild once again by engulfing him in her wet heat, riding him with a slow rolling motion that had robbed him of whatever wits she hadn't already stolen. When he finally came, the intensity of his climax had practically blown his head from his shoulders.

After wringing him out like a dishrag, she'd pulled the covers over them, wrapping them in a cocoon of warmth and snuggled against him. It was the last thing he remembered until Paolo's voice had awakened him.

And now that he was awake, he immediately wanted to see her. Touch her. Talk to her. Kiss her. Make love to her.

A huff of wry amusement puffed past his lips. Man, he really had it bad. Now he knew exactly what his dad meant when he'd described that first meeting with Mom. *Bang.* That was it.

Like father, like son.

Brett reached out and brushed his hand over the empty space where she'd slept, the place where she belonged, and disappointment filled him. Not only because he simply missed having there, but also because he'd planned to talk to her this morning about continuing their relationship once they arrived home.

For him it was a no-brainer, and he assumed she felt the same way, but he wanted to make sure she clearly understood that as far as he was concerned, this wasn't simply an adrenaline-rush vacation fling. He figured he'd wait to drop the I-love-you bomb, but he planned to make his desire to continue seeing her clear.

Oh, well, plenty of time to discuss that. And glean some pertinent information from her—like her phone number and address.

Unable to wait any longer, he dressed quickly, then headed toward the kitchen tent. Kayla met him midway, greeting him with a smile and a cup of coffee.

"Good morning, sleepyhead," she said, handing him the steaming mug. "I was just heading back to the tent to bring you this."

"Thank you. And good morning." He brushed his lips over hers, nearly laughing at the heat that zoomed through him at the casual contact. "Any oversleeping on my part is completely your fault."

She raised her brows. "Is that a complaint?"

"Hell, no." He wrapped his free arm around her waist and pulled her against him. "My only complaint is that you weren't there when I woke up. I missed you."

"I…I couldn't sleep, so when I caught the first whiff of coffee, I figured I'd get dressed and score us some java."

He leaned back and searched her face, noting even in the dim light the smudges beneath her eyes. "Couldn't sleep? You feel okay?"

She smiled. "I'm fine. My mind is just full. Lots of thoughts, all whirling around."

"Well, sweetheart, you *emptied* my mind last night." He nudged his pelvis against hers. "Among other things. If Paolo hadn't shouted out the rise-and-shine call, I probably would have slept for a week. I intend to write the author of *Mastering the Art of the Erotic Massage* a heartfelt thank-you note."

She laughed and nudged him back. "The pleasure was mine."

"Not entirely, I can promise you that."

"I think we're both all paid up now. You owed me pleasure—twice—because you cheated and let me win our bet, and I owed you an erotic massage. We're even."

He shook his head. "I seem to recall a mention of

make-up sex in there somewhere which hasn't happened yet. So you still owe me one."

"Not that I mind being indebted to you, but the only way we can have make-up sex is if we get into an argument." She rose on her toes and gently bit his earlobe, rushing more blood straight to his groin. "And arguing isn't exactly what I had in mind."

Unfortunately Paolo chose that moment to walk by and clap him on the back. "Glad to see you finally dragged it out of bed, *señor.* Breakfast in five minutes, then we need to pack up quickly if we're to arrive at Machu Picchu with the sun."

"Five minutes," Brett said with a groan. "Not nearly enough time for what *I* had in mind."

"Me, either."

He dropped a quick kiss to her upturned lips. "Hold that thought. At least until we've checked into our hotel this afternoon."

The rest of the campers slowly exited their tents, all anxious for coffee. While they enjoyed their breakfast, Paolo filled them in on some of Machu Picchu's history.

"The legendary lost city of the Incas was rediscovered in 1911 by an American team of archaeologists from Yale University led by Hiram Bingham. Of course, like most men, Mr. Bingham didn't ask for directions and was actually looking for Vilcabamba, a stronghold of the Inca rebels, when he discovered Machu Picchu, and was convinced he'd been successful.

"Since the Incas didn't leave written records, Machu Picchu remains shrouded in mystery. Some believe it was a sanctuary inhabited by high priests, others feel it was used for astronomical studies. Other theories include agricultural site and citadel. Or perhaps it is a combination of all or some of those. Most mysterious of all is that in spite of the exceedingly fine construction and architecture, Machu Picchu was built, inhabited and abandoned all in the span of less than a century—a tiny blip in time considering the four-thousand-year history of Peru. Today scholars still ask *why?*"

Paolo sipped his coffee, then continued, "Some suggest it was the result of wars between rival Inca tribes resulting in the mass execution of the entire community. Or perhaps it was a plague. Given the site's pristine condition, scholars agree that it is unlikely that the Spanish conquistadors ever found Machu Picchu during their invasions as they made no mention of it in their meticulous chronicles."

After finishing their meal, the group packed up their belongings and set out on the final leg of their journey, which, they found thankfully, was shorter and not as strenuous as the previous days' hikes. They followed a broad, level path which wound gently through light woodland, the air cool and still. With the first streaks of light in the sky, their walkway was dappled with color from scores of butterflies flitting across the trail.

They arrived at Intipunku, the Sun Gate, a short time later. After a final, thigh-murdering, fifty-step, nearly vertical climb that left them all gasping, suddenly the whole of Machu Picchu was spread before them, in all its enigmatic glory, captured in the glowing splendor of the golden rays of the sunrise.

Brett stared at the fantastic sight, at the incredible series of terraces and buildings nestled amongst the verdant landscape, and he felt as if he'd stepped back in time. He reached out and entwined his fingers with Kayla's.

She gently squeezed his hand, then whispered, "It's even more impressive than I'd envisioned. I'm almost expecting an ancient Inca warrior wearing full ceremonial dress to step from an archway."

They spent the day exploring the ruins, from the Temple of the Sun with its extraordinary stonework which fitted together seamlessly, an incomprehensible achievement for a people who had neither a written language nor the wheel, to the Temple of the Moon, a place of mysterious caverns with a carved throne and altar.

Hours later, as the sun disappeared behind the snow-capped peaks in the distance, the group headed toward the guard post where they would exit. Everyone except Brett and Kayla, who were spending the night at the Sanctuary Lodge, were heading to the train station in nearby Aguas Calientes to travel back to Cusco. Once outside the gate, there was a hasty exchange of e-mail addresses along with promises to keep in touch and e-mail photos. Then hugs and handshakes all around as the people who had come to mean so much to Brett over such a short period of time departed and went on with their lives, filling him with sorrow that he wouldn't be seeing them again tomorrow. Their adventure together was over.

But speaking of people who'd come to mean a lot to him in a short period of time…

His gaze settled on Kayla and when she looked at him, her bottom lip trembled.

"I'm going to miss them," she said with a catch in her voice.

He drew her into his arms and she rested her forehead against his chest. "Me, too. But hey, I'm glad that at least

I won't have to miss *you.* Pretty great that we live in the same city."

A strangled sound came from her. Burying her face against his neck, her shoulders shook and she sobbed as if her heart were breaking.

Not certain how to comfort her, he just held her, brushing his lips over her temple, murmuring reassurances that everything would be fine, that they'd keep in touch with everyone, and waited for the storm to pass.

When it seemed the worst was over, he pulled a hanky from his jeans' pocket and handed it to her. "Don't worry—it's a clean one," he said with a smile.

She looked up at him, her green eyes wet with tears, her lashes spiky, and whatever small part of his heart might have remained his own, he lost with that single look.

"I'm sorry," she said, after giving her nose a lusty blow.

"No problem." He chucked her gently under the chin and grinned. "But I've gotta tell ya, for a woman who claimed she wasn't a weepy female, you sure do cry a lot. And it is *not* easy on a guy's nerves."

"Or his hankies," she said with a wobbly smile.

"I have plenty." He cradled her tearstained face between his hands and brushed at the wetness lingering on her cheeks with his thumbs. "Feel better?"

For several long seconds she simply looked at him with an unreadable expression and he wished like hell he knew what she was thinking.

Finally she jerked her head in a nod. "Better." Then she grimaced. "But I know for sure I'm not *looking* better. I must be a total mess."

"You look beautiful."

A watery laugh huffed from her lips. "That's very

sweet, but I know what I look like when I cry. Blotchy skin, red nose, swollen eyes. It ain't pretty."

"You're right. It's beautiful." He leaned down and lightly kissed her lips. "I can't wait to get you alone in our hotel room so I can show you just how beautiful."

Another huff of laughter. "I'm hideous. With the way I look, you cannot possibly be turned on."

"Yet this," he lightly bumped her with the obvious bulge in his jeans, "suggests I am."

"Good heavens." She swiped beneath her eyes with the hanky again. "Are you always this horny?"

His gaze rested on hers, all vestiges of amusement gone, and he shook his head. "No. Just with you. Only you."

Her lips trembled and with no small amount of alarm he saw her eyes puddling up again. "Okay, that's it for you, Miss Waterworks. I'm getting you to the hotel. Now. Before I have to dig another hanky out of my backpack."

Thirty minutes later they walked down the hallway toward their room at the Machu Picchu Sanctuary Lodge, the hotel perched right next to the ruins. Kayla had had her own room reserved, but they'd cancelled the reservation when checking in as they only needed one. And by God, he couldn't wait much longer to get to it. And judging by the way she rubbed herself against him while he tried to unlock the damn door, neither could she.

When he finally closed the door behind them, they dropped their backpacks and fell on each other as if they were starved and had suddenly been offered a feast.

"Hope your heart isn't set on slow and easy." He yanked her sweatshirt over her head with a lack of finesse that probably should have appalled him.

"Do I *look* like I want slow and easy?" she asked, jerking his T-shirt from his jeans with the same haste he'd exhibited. With her eyes, darkened with arousal, steady on his, she flicked open the button on his jeans then lowered the zipper. Wrapping her fingers around his straining erection, she said, "This morning you told me to 'hold that thought' and I've held it all day. Now I want to see what you intend to do about it. And I want to see it hard and fast. Any complaints?"

"Hell, no." Nothing not to love about a woman who wasn't afraid to ask for what she wanted. And even better when he wanted the same thing.

Amidst much kissing and panting and groping and laughing and digging through backpacks for condoms, they tugged off boots and jeans and underwear then tumbled onto the bed. Settling himself between her splayed thighs, he wasted no time giving her what she wanted, what they both wanted—hard and fast. After a wild, furious ride that left them spent, he lifted her arms above her head, entwined their fingers, and looked into her slumberous eyes. And saw everything he'd ever wanted.

"You do hard and fast *very* well," she murmured.

"So do you. For my encore performance, how do you feel about sharing a nice, hot bath in our very own indoor bathroom?"

Her eyes widened. "The fact that you made me forget, for even one second, let alone long enough to make love, that such a luxury was within reach is a true testament to your appeal and skill."

He waggled his brows. "Wait 'til you see what I can do in a tubful of soapy water."

Ten minutes later, he reclined in the tub with Kayla

nestled between his spread legs, her back pressed to his chest, her temple against his chin. Her hands rested on his thighs while his fingers gently glided over her abdomen. Wisps of fragrant steam curled up from the water, filling the room with the fragrance of the hotel's orchid-scented bubble bath.

"I'm going to smell like flowers," he said, smoothing his hands over her breasts.

"Is that a problem?"

"I can stand it if you can. But it's not the most...masculine of scents."

She exhaled a long sigh filled with unmistakable pleasure. "Believe me, you don't have anything to worry about in the masculinity department."

"Glad you're pleased." He brushed a kiss over her temple, inhaling her unique scent. Which reminded him...

"You know, I've never told you about my breakthrough. Would you like to hear about it?"

He felt her stiffen in his arms. "No." The sharp word echoed in the room, then she laughed. "I mean, it's not necessary—"

He touched his finger to her lips, cutting off her words. "I know, you think it'll be a yawn-fest of chemistry mumbo-jumbo, but once you hear what this formula can do, I guarantee you won't be bored."

Holding her in his arms, he told her everything the formula could do. The anti-aging benefits. The aphrodisiac qualities. That there was nothing on the market like it. The research he'd conducted and a simplified version of the chemical process used to produce the formula's extraordinary effects. Which led to him telling her about how the cosmetics companies had hounded him to the point where, encouraged by the magazine article, he'd escaped to Peru. To get away. To decide what was best for his future, because the formula *was* his future.

When he finished, he realized she hadn't said a word through his entire recitation, or even moved.

"Hey," he said with a quiet laugh, craning his neck to kiss her cheek. "Did I bore you to sleep?"

She shook her head. "No," she replied, her voice a hoarse whisper. "I…I heard every word you said. It sounds like an incredible product."

"It is. Which is why I need to make the right decisions, and make them soon. Before all the buzz and interest wanes. Because, providing I choose wisely and trust the right people, my future will be financially set."

"Yes. It…it's always important to trust the right people."

"And after everything's fallen into place, the first order of business is sending my parents on a much-deserved vacation." He laughed. "Maybe I'll send them to Machu Picchu."

Instead of laughing with him, she sat up and turned around to face him. There was something in her eyes, something bleak, but before he could question her, she wrapped her arms around his neck and kissed him. Like she meant it. With an urgency that felt like desperation. Which was fine by him.

By the time she let him come up for air, his head was spinning.

"Make love to me, Brett," she whispered, peppering his jaw with fevered kisses. "Now. Please."

He was only too happy to comply. Then, and twice

more throughout the evening before they finally fell asleep wrapped in each other's arms.

When he awoke the next morning, he reached out for her. But instead of finding her warm body, he found only an empty space. Eyes still closed, a smile quirked his lips. Probably the princess was enjoying the indoor plumbing.

After a few minutes passed without any sound coming from the bathroom, he called out "Kayla?"

Only more silence greeted him.

Pushing up onto his elbow, he blinked against the early-morning sunshine slanting through the windows. He was about to call her name again when his gaze fell on the pillow where she'd slept next to him.

And stared at an envelope bearing his name.

He stilled, then his gaze shifted around the room.

All traces of her were gone.

Her backpack, her clothes that had lain scattered across the floor. The lotion she'd set on the nightstand.

His gaze jerked back to the envelope, and a sick feeling gripped him, his every instinct screaming that he wasn't going to like what he read. As if in a trance, he reached for the envelope. Unfolded the letter. Read her words.

When Brett finished, his hand fisted, crumpling the paper, which he then heaved across the room. After the wadded paper hit the wall, it fell to the floor.

Where it joined his shattered heart.

21

KAYLA SAT in the stretch limo next to Meg and adjusted her sister's voluminous bridal veil. Their mother sat across from them, blotting her eyes which had sprung a leak the minute she'd seen Meg in her wedding gown. Cindy was practicing deep breathing to stave off the motion sickness she suffered along with morning sickness. Meg had threatened to sue her if she hurled in the limo and Kayla wasn't sure that Meg was kidding. After all the exhausting preparations that had gone into this wedding, by God, no one, preggers or not, better have the nerve to barf.

Well, after today, Bridezilla would be married and, with any luck, after a two-week honeymoon in Hawaii, Meg would revert back to being merely a type A personality, as opposed to insanely type-A plus.

"Are you all right, Kayla?" her mom asked, peering at her through watery eyes. "You haven't seemed like yourself lately, dear. Not since you returned from South America. Oh, I hope you didn't pick up one of those viruses you read about in the paper."

"I'm fine, Mom," Kayla lied. She was actually the exact opposite of fine, but she didn't want to talk about it. Certainly not here and now. Maybe after the wedding was over, but really what was there to say? Girl met perfect boy with whom she fell madly, passionately in love. Girl was lying idiot and lost perfect boy. Girl now wallowing in lonely misery of her own making.

Because she had absolutely lost him.

She'd left him in that hotel room with that letter exactly one month ago. While her common sense had told her she'd never hear from him again, her heart...her foolish, head-over-heels-in-love heart had continued to hold on to a thread of hope that he'd understand. Forgive her. Still want her in spite of what she'd written to him.

But as the days had turned into weeks, her heart had slowly crumbled, turning to dust. Of course he didn't understand. Of course he didn't forgive her.

Of course he didn't still want her.

Why would he? He could have any woman he wanted. For a short, magical time, *she* was the one he'd wanted. But that time had passed, and she needed to move on.

But, good God, it was so difficult to do so when every time she thought of him it hurt to breathe. And she thought about him *all the time.*

Of course, the wedding preparations *had* kept her busy for the last miserable month—very helpful since she didn't have anything else to occupy her time or thoughts. After today, she wouldn't even have the Great Bridal Diversion to distract her any longer. No, she'd just have lots of free time. Free time with nothing to do but think about Brett.

"You know, there's going to be a lot of eligible men at the wedding." Her mother gave her an encouraging nod. "You might find Mr. Right amongst Robert's scads of single lawyer friends."

"Just double-check with me before you agree to date any of them," Meg said. "There are a few who have out-of-state girlfriends they conveniently forget to mention when they're not around."

"Thanks for the warning," Kayla said, turning to look out the tinted window at the busy Manhattan street, "but I'm not looking."

"Which is exactly when you find Mr. Right," her mom said in her mother-knows-best voice.

Too late. Found him. Lost him. Can we please move on?

"Well, next week, you and Cindy and I will go shoe-shopping together," Mom said. "That'll cheer you up."

"Don't wanna go shoe-shopping," Cindy roused herself to say. "Wanna sleep. Wanna not barf."

"We *all* want you to not barf," Meg informed her in a lawyerly voice that no doubt wrung confessions from hardened criminals. "In fact, I *forbid* you to barf."

Kayla forced a smile for her mother's benefit. "Shoe-shopping sounds…" *Exhausting.* And like a total waste of time. Given her situation, she couldn't afford to splurge on footwear she didn't need. "…like fun."

The limo stopped at a light and Kayla saw Delriccio's bakery on the corner. Just something else that had gone wrong lately. Every time she'd visited the bakery this past week they'd been completely sold out of her favorite hand-dipped double chocolate chunk biscotti. Jeez. On top of being utterly miserable, she was going through biscotti withdrawal. Of course, being sold out of the double chocolate chunk was probably a good thing, since her Vera Wang maid-of-honor gown was feeling a tad snug, thanks to all the pity-party biscotti she'd consumed during the last month.

She shifted and grimaced at the zipper pinching into her back. Okay, fine, her dress was more than a *tad* snug. She'd barely gotten the damn zipper up. Even pregnant Cindy looked less pudgy. She lived in fear of drawing too deep a breath and splitting her Wang from seam to seam. If the mortification of that didn't kill her, Meg surely would, for ruining the wedding.

But, as miserable as she was, what difference did a few extra inches around her waist and some cellulite on her ass matter? Oh, right, don't forget to toss in the trio of zits on her forehead. They just perfectly closed the deal.

She glanced at her watch. Only about ten or eleven more hours in the tight dress and uncomfortable shoes. Then she could go home and crawl back into bed and pull the covers over her head.

Arriving at the church, Kayla had little to do before the ceremony began, since Meg had seen to it that every detail was taken care of. In spite of Meg's tendency to be bossy, Kayla couldn't help but admire her formidable sister. She'd known what she wanted and had gone after it and planned her perfect wedding and that's all there was to it.

So she was surprised when, just before they were to line up to walk down the aisle, Meg turned to her and asked in an uncertain voice, "It's all good, right, Kayla?"

Kayla reached out and squeezed her hand. "Meg, everything is absolutely perfect."

Walking down the aisle, Kayla held her head high and smiled at the assembled friends and relatives, forcing herself to concentrate on Meg's happiness and not her own misery. And to not breathe in too deeply—lest she and Vera Wang suffer an unfortunate parting of the ways.

The ceremony was beautiful, from the flowers to the words to the music. Listening to Meg and Robert exchange vows, their love for each other so obvious, tears gathered in Kayla's eyes. Tears of envy because she wanted what they had—minus all the Bridezilla stuff, of course. Tears of joy because she was genuinely happy for her sister. And tears of loss because she'd lost a man who'd once looked at her through golden-brown eyes filled with the same sort of warmth and admiration shining in the groom's eyes for his bride.

After the ceremony and receiving line, the bridal party assembled in the church for pictures. Endless pictures. Good God, how many pictures could they take?

Then the picture taking moved outside. Posing on the church steps. More photos. Thank goodness Meg had refused to allow the traditional rice or bird seed to be tossed. Instead everyone held tiny little bottles of bubbles, and when the signal was given, they all blew out a stream of bubbles, engulfing the bride and groom in thousands of delicate soap spheres that floated up with the warm summer breeze.

Meg and Robert ran amongst the bubbles to the white antique Rolls Royce that would transport them to Central Park for more pictures, then onto the Waldorf Astoria for the reception. The rest of the bridal party would meet them at the Waldorf, traveling in style in the stretch limo. And once they arrived, they'd be subjected to more picture taking.

The crowd slowly dispersed, and Kayla stood on the top step, chatting with her cousin Daniel who lived in Florida, and whom she hadn't seen in five years. He was talking about some night club he'd invested in and even though she nodded politely, her attention wandered to the people milling around on the steps and sidewalk. Uncle Will and Aunt Gwen were chatting with her mom and Cindy. Meg's boss and his wife were talking to a young couple Kayla didn't know. Cousins Debbie and Marla. Another couple Kayla didn't recognize. Brett Thornton.

She went perfectly still, then blinked twice, certain she was seeing wrong.

But there was no mistake. Brett stood on the sidewalk below, looking up the stairs, his gaze fixed on her.

For several stunned seconds she couldn't move. Couldn't breathe. Could only stare. For one crazy instant she thought he was a guest—some cruel trick of fate that he somehow knew Meg or Robert and had been invited to the wedding, not realizing the bride was her sister.

But no, he was dressed casually in jeans and a short-sleeved shirt.

Her heart jumped back to life and she reached out to grip the banister lest her trembling legs gave out. Afraid to so much as blink, in case he was some sort of mental mirage brought on by misery and biscotti deprivation, she excused herself to Daniel, then moved down one cautious step. When Brett didn't disappear, she risked another, then another.

His gaze never moved from her, and she continued with her jerky steps. When she passed by where her mother stood, Kayla heard her ask, "Honey, are you okay?"

She nodded. At least she thought she did. She tried to. She could feel the weight of her mother's stare on her back, but she didn't stop. Didn't pause until only six feet separated her and Brett. And then, wouldn't you know it, her throat slammed shut. She had to swallow three times to find her voice, and then only managed to say, "Hi" in a high-pitched voice she didn't recognize.

"Hello, Kayla."

A breath she hadn't realized she was holding whooshed from her lungs. Until he'd spoken, part of her had really wondered if he might be a mirage.

"Wh-what are you doing here? Out for a walk?"

"No." He regarded her through very serious eyes. "I came here to see you."

Oh, God, she was going to fall down. Right here, on the sidewalk. After locking her shaky knees, she wet her lips then said, "You did?"

"I did. I've been trying to get in touch with you for the past week, but since we'd never exchanged phone numbers or addresses and you're unlisted, it's been challenging." He slipped his hands into his back pockets and she pressed her lips together, trying to force back the memory of those talented hands skimming down her body. Gently framing her face.

"I tried to find you through La Fleur, but when I called the company, all the receptionist would tell me is that you don't work there anymore."

She nodded. "That's correct. I don't."

He studied her for several seconds, and she wondered what he was thinking. "Then I remembered about your sister getting married. I checked the announcements in the *Times,* and found the name *Watson,* saw that the wedding was here, today. And here I am."

Yes, and here he was. Looking so big and strong and gorgeous she wanted to throw herself into his arms. And staring at her with an unreadable expression that had her heart jumping in her chest.

"It's good to see you," she whispered, appalled when her voice broke on the last word. She offered up a quick prayer to the Patron Saint of Tissues to please not let her cry. Surely such a simple prayer could be answered, seeing as how they stood right outside a church.

"Do you have a few minutes?" he asked. "Or do you need to leave right now?"

"I have some time. Meg and Robert are going to stop in the park for a few pictures," she looked skyward, "or a few hundred pictures, before going to the Waldorf."

The ghost of a smile touched his lips, and her breath hitched at the suggestion of the dimple in his cheek. He nodded toward the church. "Do you think we could sit in there and talk?"

"I don't see why not. It's not as if there aren't plenty of seats."

She turned and started up the stairs, carefully lifting the hem of her Wang because of all the times to go splat, this would be a really bad one. She heard him climbing the stone steps behind her and an image of them hiking the trail flashed through her mind, of his teasing smile as he ogled her butt.

She strongly doubted he was ogling her now. In fact she hoped he wasn't, because if he was, he'd surely notice that there was more to ogle.

As she neared her mother and Cindy, both of whose avid glances were bouncing between her and Brett, she shot them a please-don't-ask look and said, "I'll be along soon. Don't wait the limo for me. I'll just grab a cab and meet you at the Waldorf."

And then, in case they missed the don't-ask look, she kept on climbing, not wanting to perform introductions to a man they'd never see again. As it was, she'd have to field dozens of questions the moment she arrived at the reception.

"Who's that man with Kayla?" she heard Cindy whisper to their mother. Unfortunately, Cindy didn't know *how* to whisper, and when she tried, she was invariably louder than if she'd just spoken normally.

"I don't know, but it's my guess he's the reason she's been so distraught," answered Mom, in the same loud whisper she'd passed along the gene pool to Cindy.

"She's been distraught?"

"Oh, yes, dear. Ever since she returned from Peru. You've just been too busy barfing to notice."

Kayla winced and kept climbing, trapped from sprinting up the steps by her high heels and tight Wang.

After passing through the vestibule, Kayla led the way into the empty church, then slid into the last pew, relieved to be off her feet. Brett sat next to her, turning sideways in the seat to face her, then setting a shiny blue shopping bag on the floor. Where had that come from? Obviously he'd had it all along and she just hadn't noticed. Not surprising, given her shock at seeing him.

The last thing she wanted was to look into those golden-brown eyes that had once regarded her with desire, knowing that no longer seeing it would hurt. But she owed him the courtesy of meeting his gaze.

And when she did, her heart hurt at the unreadable expression with which he regarded her. Well, she supposed she deserved this. For whatever reason, he obviously wanted to have it out face to face, so she might as well get it over with.

"What did you want to talk about, Brett?"

"A lot of things. But first, I want to know about your job. Why don't you work at La Fleur anymore?"

"Does it matter?"

"I wouldn't ask if it didn't." He frowned. "Did you lose your job because of me?"

"No."

He looked...surprised? "I'd like to know what happened, Kayla," he said quietly.

She hesitated, then, looking down at her hands, said, "Very well. I resigned. I gave my two-week notice the day I returned from Peru."

Silence greeted her answer, then one quiet word. "Why?"

She looked up and again met his gaze. "Because I couldn't look at myself in the mirror. Because I was ashamed of my boss for expecting me to spy on you and of myself for agreeing to do so. I no longer wanted to be involved in any way with anything to do with your formula, so I took myself out of the game."

"By resigning."

"Yes."

"So you don't have a job?"

"I don't." She lifted her chin. "But I have my integrity and self-respect back, or at least I'm working on it. Unfortunately they don't pay the rent, but I have a few promising prospects lined up." She paused, then said, "I want you to know...I didn't repeat anything you said about your formula to my boss. I know you don't have any reason to believe me but—"

"I believe you."

Those three softly spoken words stilled her and

she pressed her hands together so he wouldn't see them trembling.

"Thank you. That's more than I deserve."

She waited for him to say something, anything, but when the silence swelled and he merely kept looking at her, a frown bunching his brows while his gaze roamed her features, she finally asked, "Why had you wanted to get in touch with me?"

Instead of answering, he said, "That woman, on the stairs, was she your mother?"

"Yes. And my sister, Cindy."

"Your mother said you'd been distraught ever since you came home from Peru."

She shrugged. "You know how moms are."

"She seemed to think the reason you were distraught was because of a man."

"Mom doesn't know I resigned from my job. Neither do my sisters. I didn't want to tell them before the wedding because they'd only worry and ask ten thousand questions I didn't feel up to answering."

His gaze pinned hers. "So the reason you've been distraught has only to do with leaving your job?"

"Actually, that has nothing to do with it. I'm not now, nor have I been, distraught over leaving my job, Brett. I have no regrets in regard to that decision."

"Then why have you been upset?"

"You can't figure it out?"

"I'd prefer that you tell me."

She again looked down at her hands, digging deep for courage, then raised her head to meet his gaze. "All right. You deserve the words. I've been distraught because I fell in love with you. And because of my actions, I lost you.

I'm hoping that someday I won't feel quite so distraught, but that day hasn't come yet. I can tell you it's not today. Tomorrow's not looking real good, either."

She drew another bracing breath. "And even though I explained everything in my letter and tried to tell you how sorry I was, you also deserve a face-to-face apology. I'm sorry, Brett. I deeply regret my reasons for going to Peru and can only reiterate that those reasons had *nothing* to do with my attraction to you or my decision to sleep with you or the feelings I developed for you."

A muscle ticked in his jaw. "Thank you for that. I can't deny that finding you gone, leaving only that letter...hurt me."

"I'm sorry. That's the last thing I wanted."

"I think the fact that you left, that you told me in a letter instead of staying and telling me face to face, hurt more than the actual contents of the letter."

She shook her head. "Just another selfish act on my part. I couldn't stand the thought of all the affection I'd seen in your eyes disappearing."

"That was more than affection, Kayla. I'd fallen in love with you, too."

His words pierced her already aching heart, hurt echoing from his use of the past tense.

"Why didn't you tell me about resigning from your job?" he asked.

"We haven't exactly kept in touch."

"You didn't mention in your letter that you intended to do so."

"No. Actually, I didn't want you to know. It was my own personal...penance of sorts. Please don't worry about it. As I said, I have no regrets. At least about that."

The church bells chimed, marking the half hour, and she knew she needed to leave soon. "You never told me why you'd wanted to get in touch with me."

"I wanted to see you. Talk to you. For the first three weeks I was home, I was very hurt. And very angry. At you. At what you'd done. And then for leaving me like that. I stalked around like a lion with a thorn in its paw, telling myself I was better off without you, that I didn't care, that it didn't matter.

"I threw myself into finding the right lawyer to represent me, to deciding the best thing to do with my formula. And I finally decided."

When she remained silent he asked, "Don't you want to know?"

"Only if you want to tell me."

"I signed a contract two days ago with Parisian Cosmetics."

She nodded slowly. "Small company based in France, very high-end products, sold only in the most exclusive shops." She smiled. "Congratulations."

He smiled in return. "Thank you."

"Will you be sending your parents to Machu Picchu?"

"I wanted to. They'd rather go to Vegas. Go figure."

"So *no change, no gain* worked out well for you. I guess your life's now back in balance."

"Not entirely." His expression sobered, and he reached out and gently took her hand. "I read your note over and over, until I could recite the words without even looking at it. And after the initial anger and hurt settled down a bit, all I could see when I read that letter was how sorry you were. How bad you felt. How deeply you regretted your actions."

He blew out a quick breath. "Hell, I've done plenty of things that I regretted. Lots of stuff I was sorry for. That's when my anger and hurt started to fade and the only thing left was…loneliness."

The pad of his thumb brushed over the back of her hand and tingles zoomed up her arm. "I finally decided that there was one more risk I had to take, and it involved you. I wanted, needed to see you. Talk to you. To find out what had happened with your boss when you returned."

His compelling gaze rested on hers. "It never occurred to me that you'd resign from your job, but the fact that you did…well, it just proves what I knew, what I finally figured out. That you are the woman I knew you were, from the first moment I saw you.

"Kayla, a good person isn't someone who never makes a mistake. It's someone who admits to them. Who apologizes and tries to make amends. A person who'd leave their job, rather than allow it to compromise them."

"I did allow it to."

"But not for long. So you're not perfect. Here's a news flash—neither am I." His lopsided grin flashed. "You heard it here first. And there was one more reason I wanted to see you. I wanted to know if you'd been as unhappy as I was."

"I've been *really* unhappy," she said in a shaky voice, and then, to her utter mortification, tears spilled from her eyes, running down her cheeks and plopping on her Vera Wang. "I've done nothing but mope and cry," she said, each word punctuated with a juicy sob and more tears, "and eat biscotti and I've gained weight and my butt is fat and my dress is tight and I've missed you so much it hurts to breathe—even without this damn tight dress."

He whipped a hanky from his back pocket and with a tender smile, dabbed at her eyes.

"And now Meg is going to yell because I'll look all blotchy in the pictures and have tear stains on my Wang."

"On your what?"

"My Wang. My dress."

"Oh. That's a…relief. You women have the darnedest names for clothes. And you don't look blotchy. You're beautiful," he said, blotting her eyes. "And you're not fat, either."

"I know you're just saying that, but thank you anyway."

"I'm not just saying it. You look gorgeous." He cradled her damp face between his hands. "Did you mean it when you said that you'd fallen in love with me?"

"Yes." She briefly closed her eyes. "God, yes."

"Have your feelings changed?"

She gave a jerky nod. "They've grown stronger."

There was no mistaking the relief that filled his eyes. "Well, that's good news. Because I love you, Kayla. It was a done deal for me from moment one."

Resting her hands over his, she let the tears dribble down her cheeks unchecked. "Thank you for forgiving me."

"Thank you for loving me."

A happy laugh escaped her. "Trust me, it's very easy to do."

He leaned forward and kissed her, a lush, deep kiss filled with love and heat and passion that left her breathless. When he lifted his head, she felt decidedly dazed. "Wow. That's potent. And probably very inappropriate given our location."

"You're right. But you make me forget where I am."

He glanced down then shook his head. "*And* what I'm doing. I almost forgot. I brought you a present." He handed her the large blue shopping bag.

"What is it?"

He smiled. "Bet you'd find out if you looked inside."

She opened the bag and stared. At what appeared to be dozens of—

"Biscotti?" she murmured, pulling one out. Then her eyes widened. "And not just any biscotti. These are Delriccio's hand-dipped double chocolate chunk biscotti."

"They are indeed."

"Where did you get them?"

"Uh, Delriccio's."

"But how? They've been sold out of them this entire week!"

"I know." He nodded toward the bag and grinned. "Who do you think bought them all?"

Her jaw dropped. "You have—single handedly—bought out Delriccio's supply of hand-dipped double chocolate chunk biscotti for an entire *week?*"

"I remembered they were your favorite. I went in every morning before work, hoping to see you there."

"Since I left my job, I've been going in the afternoon." She gazed again into the bag. "There must be at least a hundred of them in here."

"Maybe a few less. I ate a couple—dozen. They're really good."

"Don't I know it. I've been suffering withdrawal all week." She groaned. "If I eat even one of these, I'll never fit in this dress again."

He trailed nipping kisses along her jaw, then

swooped in for another deep, lush kiss. When he lifted his head, he said, "I don't mind if you take it off."

A giggle erupted from her. "We're in a *church.*"

"Right. See? You made me forget again." His gaze wandered over her dress. "So, do you, uh, have a date for the wedding?"

"No."

"Why not?"

"There was only one person I wanted to bring and he was…unavailable."

"Oh? You asked him?"

"No…and I'd love for him to come, but if he did, he'd have to brace himself to not only meet my entire family, but to suffer through what I'm sure would feel like an interrogation from all the relatives."

"I think he could cope. I bet he could even dash home and change into his tux and be back at the Waldorf within an hour."

She looped her arms around his neck. "Have I mentioned that I love you?"

"Not in the last five minutes."

"I love you."

"Excellent. Because I love you, too."

Kayla drew a deep breath then groaned as her Wang squeezed her. "God, I can't wait to get out this dress."

"That makes two of us."

She shot him a speculative look. "You know, if we hurry, I could go with you to your apartment to change…"

Without hesitation he jumped to his feet, grabbed her hand and the shopping bag, and walked swiftly toward the doors. "Sweetheart, I like the way you think."

"Not so fast," she said, taking mincing steps and

holding up her hem. “I’m not exactly wearing my hiking boots here.”

Again, without hesitation, he bent and swooped her up into his arms, shopping bag and all, then headed out of the church.

“You can’t carry me down all those stairs,” she said, wrapping her arms around his neck.

“The hell I can’t.” He paused at the top of the steps, then looked down at her, his beautiful eyes filled with desire and love. “Me carrying you—is that a complaint, princess?”

“Hell, no,” she said with a laugh, then snuggled closer against him. “Hell, no.”

* * * * *

Set in darkness beyond the ordinary world.
Passionate tales of life and death.
With characters' lives ruled by laws the everyday world can't begin to imagine.

Introducing NOCTURNE, *a spine-tingling new line from Silhouette Books.*

The thrills and chills begin with UNFORGIVEN by Lindsay McKenna

Plucked from the depths of hell, former military sharpshooter Reno Manchahi was hired by the government to kill a thief, but he had a mission of his own. Descended from a family of shape-shifters, Reno vowed to get the revenge he'd thirsted for all these years. But his mission went awry when his target turned out to be a powerful seductress, Magdalena Calen Hernandez, who risked everything to battle a potent evil. Suddenly, Reno had to transform himself into a true hero and fight the enemy that threatened them all. He had to become a Warrior for the Light….

Turn the page for a sneak preview of UNFORGIVEN by Lindsay McKenna.
On sale September 26, wherever books are sold.

Chapter 1

One shot...one kill.

The sixteen-pound sledgehammer came down with such fierce power that the granite boulder shattered instantly. A spray of glittering mica exploded into the air and sparkled momentarily around the man who wielded the tool as if it were a weapon. Sweat ran in rivulets down Reno Manchahi's drawn, intense face. Naked from the waist up, the hot July sun beating down on his back, he hefted the sledgehammer skyward once more. Muscles in his thick forearms leaped and biceps bulged. Even his breath was focused on the boulder. In his mind's eye, he pictured Army General Robert Hampton's fleshy, arrogant fifty-year-old features on the rock's surface. Air exploded from between his lips as he brought the avenging hammer down. The boulder pulverized beneath his funneled hatred.

One shot...one kill...

Nostrils flaring, he inhaled the dank, humid heat and drew it deep into his massive lungs. Revenge allowed Reno to endure his imprisonment at a U.S. Navy brig near San Diego, California. Drops of sweat were flung in all directions as the crack of his sledgehammer claimed a third stone victim. Mouth taut, Reno moved to the next boulder.

The other prisoners in the stone yard gave him a wide berth. They always did. They instinctively felt his simmering hatred, the palpable revenge in his cinnamon-colored eyes, was more than skin-deep.

And they whispered he was different.

Reno enjoyed being a loner for good reason. He came from a medicine family of shape-shifters. But even this secret power had not protected him—or his family. His wife, Ilona, and his three-year-old daughter, Sarah, were dead. Murdered by Army General Hampton in their former home on USMC base in Camp Pendleton, California. Bitterness thrummed through Reno as he savagely pushed the toe of his scarred leather boot against several smaller pieces of gray granite that were in his way.

The sun beat down upon Manchahi's naked shoulders, grown dark red over time, shouting his half-Apache heritage. With his straight black hair grazing his thick shoulders, copper skin and broad face with high cheekbones, everyone knew he was Indian. When he'd first arrived at the brig, some of the prisoners taunted him and called him Geronimo. Something strange happened to Reno during his fight with the name-calling prisoners. Leaning down after he'd won the scuffle, he'd snarled into each of their bloodied faces that if they were going to call him anything, they would call him *gan,* which was the Apache word for *devil.*

His attackers had been shocked by the wounds on their faces, the deep claw marks. Reno recalled doubling his fist as they'd attacked him en masse. In that split second, he'd gone into an altered state of consciousness.

In times of danger, he transformed into a jaguar. A deep, growling sound had emitted from his throat as he defended himself in the three-against-one fracas. It all happened so fast that he thought he had imagined it. He'd seen his hands morph into a forearm and paw, claws extended. The slashes left on the three men's faces after the fight told him he'd begun to shape-shift. A fist made bruises and swelling; not four perfect, deep claw marks. Stunned and anxious, he hid the knowledge of what else he was from these prisoners. Reno's only defense was to make all the prisoners so damned scared of him and remain a loner.

Alone. Yeah, he was alone, all right. The steel hammer swept downward with hellish ferocity. As the granite groaned in protest, Reno shut his eyes for just a moment. Sweat dripped off his nose and square chin.

Straightening, he wiped his furrowed, wet brow and looked into the pale blue sky. What got his attention was the startling cry of a red-tailed hawk as it flew over the brig yard. Squinting, he watched the bird. Reno could make out the rust-colored tail on the hawk. As a kid growing up on the Apache reservation in Arizona, Reno knew that all animals that appeared before him were messengers.

Brother, what message do you bring me? Reno knew one had to ask in order to receive. Allowing the sledgehammer to drop to his side, he concentrated on the hawk who wheeled in tightening circles above him.

Freedom! the hawk cried in return.

Reno shook his head, his black hair moving against his broad, thickset shoulders. *Freedom? No way, Brother. No way.* Figuring that he was making up the hawk's shrill message, Reno turned away. Back to his rocks. Back to picturing Hampton's smug face.

Freedom!

Look for UNFORGIVEN by Lindsay McKenna,
the spine-tingling launch title
from Silhouette Nocturne™.
Available September 26, wherever books are sold.